A Road Less Travelled

Making a Home in Saudi Arabia

Barbara Farahat

authorHOUSE®

AuthorHouse™ UK Ltd.
500 Avebury Boulevard
Central Milton Keynes, MK9 2BE
www.authorhouse.co.uk
Phone: 08001974150

©2010 Barbara Farahat. All rights reserved.

No part of this book may be reproduced, stored in a retrieval system, or transmitted by any means without the written permission of the author.

First published by AuthorHouse 5/19/2010

ISBN: 978-1-4490-6563-8 (sc)

Library of Congress Control Number: 2010906694

This book is printed on acid-free paper.

For my family: without them, the road wouldn't have been worth travelling;
and
to the women who welcomed me into their lives and made me feel at home

Two roads diverged in a yellow wood,
And sorry I could not travel both
And be one traveler, long I stood
And looked down one as far as I could
To where it bent in the undergrowth;

Then took the other, as just as fair
And having perhaps the better claim,
Because it was grassy and wanted wear;
Though as for that, the passing there
Had worn them really about the same,

And both that morning equally lay
In leaves no step had trodden black
Oh, I kept the first for another day!
Yet knowing how way leads on to way,
I doubted if I should ever come back.

I shall be telling this with a sigh
Somewhere ages and ages hence:
Two roads diverged in a wood, and I,
I took the one less traveled by,
And that has made all the difference.

>   Robert Frost
>   1874–1963

Preface

A German native, I moved to Riyadh with my Saudi husband in the early seventies. Before I came to Saudi Arabia, I used to annoy the Saudis I met with my incessant questions: I wanted to know how Saudi women live. Once I moved there, I realized I knew almost nothing about the people and their customs, so I decided to have more contact with Saudi women and started working as an English teacher in the public-school sector.

My European and American friends have always asked me about my life as a woman in Saudi Arabia. Perhaps their image of the country and its people, like mine at first, was distorted. Saudi women are believed to be backwards and live in a harem-like world with no rights. The prevalence of this stereotype is one reason I decided to write a book that focuses on the lives of working Saudi women.

After 9/11, the West grew more interested in learning about Arabic countries and especially Saudi Arabia. While today more books can be found about the lives of women in Saudi Arabia, many still perpetuate negative stereotypes. I want to present a clear portrait of the daily lives of working women in Saudi Arabia: what they believe in, what they dream about, what they hope for and expect from life, and what it means to be a woman in this country. I will also touch on education, marriage customs, and the way children are raised. Finally, I shall demonstrate how the customs and the teachings of Islam dominate their lives.

1.

She woke up as the warm rays of the sun touched her face. It was hot in the backseat. Susie sat up. The sunshine lighted up the inside of their parked car. But where was Ahmed? He wasn't sleeping in the front seat. She looked around – no trace of him. It was bright outside; the desert was flat, sand as far as she could see. In some places the sand was reddish; in others it was light yellow with touches of beige. In the distance, she could see a grey line – the street. The line was almost straight. It went all the way to the horizon, where the yellow desert met the blue sky. There were no clouds, only sun.

But where was Ahmed? She couldn't see him anywhere. The motor of the car was silent; the windows and doors were locked. The key was not in the ignition. She looked around for the key and found it in the front, next to Ahmed's cup. She put the key in the ignition and opened the window.

Outside, the air was cool. A light breeze touched her face.

How peaceful the desert looks.

The sun had just risen above the horizon and now bathed everything in yellow light.

Susie got out of the car, took off her shoes, and tried to walk over the sand. The small stones were warm; ahead she saw beautiful white sand. She touched the sand and let it pearl through her fingers.

She had arrived in Saudi Arabia.

They had crossed the northern border the night before. It was dark when they entered the country. Ahmed wanted to cross the desert quickly and had continued driving straight through to get to Riyadh as soon as possible.

But where was he?

She saw something moving along the grey street at a distance. It looked like an ant, inching towards her. Soon she recognised a truck. It stopped at a street close to her; she saw Ahmed get out, talk to the driver, close the door, and then walk towards her. In his hand was a petrol container.

"Oh, you already woke up. We ran out of petrol, and I couldn't believe there wasn't a petrol station the last 200 kilometres", Ahmed said.

"I knew you'd come soon" she said. "You'd never leave me here alone in the middle of nowhere."

"I didn't know what to do about you. I can't hitchhike in Saudi Arabia with an uncovered, tall, fair, blue-eyed woman next to me; that might be dangerous. So I thought I'd let you sleep. A truck driver gave me a ride to the next petrol station; it is only 80 kilometres from here."

He filled the tank and hooted: "Let's go!"

"Look how beautiful the desert is. You never told me how beautiful and peaceful it is", Susie said.

"Just wait a bit, then you'll see how peaceful the desert really is", Ahmed replied teasingly.

They continued driving. Soon the street in front of them was glittering from the heat; the sky above reflecting on the grey asphalt surface. The desert stretched as far as the eye could see: yellow white sand and blue sky.

Ahmed stopped the black Mercedes they had bought used with their limited budget the year before in Germany.

"I have to move around a little, I'm getting tired."

He turned off the engine and opened the door. Hot, dry air hit Susie's face.

"What is this? Did somebody put us in an oven?"

"No", replied Ahmed. "This is your peaceful desert at noon."

From time to time they drove through a hamlet: a petrol station, a small shop full of cans, a few flat, small houses in the middle of nowhere. A sign posted on the outskirts of each of the villages they passed through proclaimed its name. Hardly ever did they see people walking about, and when they did they only glimpsed men; there were no women in sight. Seldom did they meet other cars; only the occasional truck passing from the opposite direction.

Susie thought about the story Ahmed had told her about his family when they first met, in Germany.

Ahmed's father, Abbas, was born in Mecca. He had built a flourishing business by manufacturing scented oil from flowers. Despite being a businessman respected by his friends and customers, he was not happy in his personal life. His wife had borne him six sons, but he had the feeling that something was missing. Abbas admired his friend Fuad, who was not as successful as he was but was very proud of his children, always talking about them, especially his eldest daughter, Fatima. Fuad used to say that Fatima was the joy of his life, his companion, the one he could always talk to whatever worries he felt.

Then, suddenly, Fuad died. Because of his longstanding friendship with Fuad, Abbas felt responsible for looking after Fuad's family. Through such circumstances, more than one opportunity arose for him to meet Fatima. Though he never saw her without her veil, in talking to her, he, too, started admiring her intelligence and her wisdom.

Abbas proposed to Fatima. In the beginning he worried about the great age difference between them and the fact that Fatima would be a second wife. But she defused his worries and told him that she would accept his proposal.

Samia was their first child. Abbas was very proud to finally have a daughter, and he spoiled her whenever Fatima gave him the opportunity. He told her that when she was old enough he would bring her private tutors to teach her reading and writing because there were no schools for girls at that time.

Then, during the month of Hajj, when Mecca was full of pilgrims from everywhere in the world, Samia developed a fever that couldn't be brought down with the available remedies. When they finally got hold of a physician, he told them that Samia had developed meningitis. The child slowly recovered, but soon Fatima noticed that she didn't react to noises. After a thorough examination, the doctor told them that Samia had lost much of her hearing.

Before long, the other daughters were born to the couple: Suad, Salwa, and Zainab. And then came Ahmed.

Even before his son started to walk, Abbas fell sick. The doctors didn't really know what was wrong with him, but since he was over sixty he was considered an old man. There were no birth certificates, and people remembered dates only in relation to special occasions – such as when Fatima's mother used to tell her that she was born in the year when they had a lot of rain after there had been a drought for many years.

A few months after falling sick, Ahmed's father died.

Because Fatima's children were still young when their father died, their eldest brother from the first wife became Fatima's and her children's guardian. From now on, he would be responsible for the well-being and the expenses of the family, and all decisions concerning the family, big or small, would be taken by him. Fatima continued living in her late husband's house just like she did when Abbas was alive: Fatima on the first floor, and the first wife, the mother of the grown-up sons, on the ground floor.

The day was winding down, and the heat had decreased in the desert. As the sun started to set, the sky slowly changed colour, until for a brief moment the empty desert was dipped in red.

"Look – how beautiful it is!" Susie said. "Did you ever see anything as beautiful?"

Ahmed laughed, "Yes, I've seen it before. Don't get too excited." Quickly, then, the darkness descended, and the moon appeared like a huge bright lantern in the sky. The night was clear, millions of stars twinkling in the firmament. It was very peaceful. Suddenly, Susie realised that all her anxiety and worries that she felt before leaving her native country, Germany, were replaced by a sense of belonging.

The next day, they reached the outskirts of Riyadh. The first houses came into sight: white, beige, grey, loam-coloured houses and walls. It all appeared like a ghost town; again, there were no people anywhere to be seen.

"Where are the people? Where are the women?" Susie asked.

"It's too early and it's summer", Ahmed replied. "Most people are still sleeping. Wait until we reach the city."

From time to time they saw a puny tree, a grey-green dot in beige-brown surroundings.

Slowly the surroundings became friendlier. They even saw some houses in cheerful colours and some green trees breaking up the endless stretch of beige sand. The houses became bigger, buildings grew taller, and the streets got cleaner.

They had arrived in Riyadh, a modern metropolis.

2.

Susie stood at the bedroom window in the apartment they shared with Ahmed's mother, Fatima, and his sister Samia. She looked down on the sand-coloured street. There were no trees. Nearby was a signal at a street corner. Cars were idling at the red light. Some drivers honked impatiently. Everybody was in a hurry. Where were they going? To work or to school? They all had a destination; they all knew what they would do during the day. Only she had nothing to do, it seemed. A day was like any other day. What was it like to work in Saudi Arabia? How did people start their day? What did they do when they arrived on the job? Would they first sit down for a chat with their colleagues, or would they start into their tasks immediately?

Probably Susie would never find out. That was another world, a world into which she could not enter. She didn't know Arabic – who would want to employ her? No one could understand her, and she didn't understand anyone.

Susie had not slept well the night before. She had had one of her recurring dreams: She was on a staircase in a dark building. She tried to climb the stairs, but suddenly the stairs stopped. With difficulty she climbed onto another staircase but still couldn't get anywhere, she was still on the same level. And again the stairs stopped. She could never reach the top, where she could see the sunlight.

Susie sighed. Would she be able to assimilate into a culture so different from her own? Or had she reached for the stars in deciding to come to Saudi Arabia, expecting to find a new home? There was so much she didn't identify with. She was about to build a family with a man from a different background and a culture she didn't understand, living in a society that was strange to her, a way of life in which she felt like a spectator and not an integral member.

As soon as Susie and Ahmed arrived in Riyadh, they went to Fatima's apartment, which would also be their home. Ahmed sent Susie up to the apartment while he got the luggage. She rang the bell. The door opened, and a small, elderly woman stood at the entrance. She had her hair loosely covered with a black scarf and was wearing a simple, colourful housedress. Her eyes were friendly.

At first, she looked at Susie with surprise, but then she realised who was standing in front of her; she took Susie into her arms and kissed her. At that moment, Ahmed arrived at the door and he kissed his mother tenderly.

Ahmed then introduced Susie to his sister Samia. Samia looked like her brother, but whereas Ahmed was handsome and well built, Samia had a smaller physique and she didn't have the warmth of her brother's face. Samia kissed Susie on both cheeks and continued preparing breakfast. Ahmed showed Susie the apartment and the bedroom, which from now on would be their private room. The rest of the apartment would be used by all of them. When they were still living in Germany, Ahmed had told Susie that she would live with his mother and his sister. Susie had always wanted a big family and didn't object to Ahmed's plan.

One by one, Ahmed's other sisters arrived, each with their families. Everybody received an affectionate greeting. They rushed to kiss and embrace Ahmed. His nieces wanted to sit close to him and jealously tried to grab his attention.

At dinnertime the family prepared to sit on the floor, since there wasn't a table big enough to seat the whole family. A tablecloth was spread on the carpet and the plates and flatware were distributed by the girls. Between each two plates they placed small bowls of salad. Ahmed's brothers-in-law put a huge plate with a cooked lamb and rice in the middle. Everybody sat down and started eating, between chatting and joking. Suad took a knife, cut the meat, and put some of it on Fatima's, Samia's, and her own daughters' plates. The men ate with their hands, whereas the women used spoons. Susie was surprised at how graceful and refined they appeared picking up the rice with their fingers.

Whenever Susie thought she was finished eating, Fatima would put another delicious piece of meat on her plate.

Salwa sat next to her young daughter and fed her, since she was still too little to eat on her own. Her sons, Tarek and Omar, sat next to their cousins on the other side of the tablecloth, whispering to one another. Mohammed, their father, told them to stop it. Immediately they obeyed and continued eating. Haifa, Suad's ten-year-old daughter, sat between her older cousins. She tried to get their attention but they ignored her. Hassan, Zainab's son, got up and left the room. Tarek and Omar wanted to follow him, but a glance from their father made them stop. Reluctantly they sat down again.

Susie felt lost. Sitting on the floor was uncomfortable for her – she didn't quite know where to put her legs. She wanted to pick up her plate and eat with the plate on her lap but felt too shy to do so.

Finally, the big plate in the middle of the tablecloth was empty; only a little rice remained of the feast.

Fatima looked at Susie and smiled. Susie couldn't help but love her mother-in-law from the first moment she saw her. She shed so much warmth and maternal protection that Susie wanted to get up, hug her, and put her head on her shoulder, but she felt inhibited about showing so much affection in front of everyone.

After the family members finished eating, they would each get up to wash their hands. When the last person finished, the girls removed all the plates and cleaned the floor.

Fruits and some small plates had been placed on a table, and after they ate the fruit, tea was served.

Everybody was having fun, teasing one another. Susie felt left out; she didn't understand what they were saying, and Ahmed, the only one she could talk to, was busy joking with his sisters, nieces, and nephews. Then Zainab's husband, Khalid, came over and sat down next to her.

"Welcome to Riyadh", he said to her in German. Susie was surprised. Ahmed laughed and explained to her that Khalid had always been interested in languages and had tried to learn a few. Not only did he speak German, he was fluent in English, Spanish, French, and Italian.

"If you are interested in German books, you are welcome to take some of mine. I'd love it if you would read them and we can then discuss the books", he told her.

Susie was delighted by Khalid's offer, but when she looked up; she noticed a jealous glance from Zainab and a hint of resentfulness in her beautiful face. So Susie only smiled at Khalid: "Thank you, that's very nice of you", and left the room to see if Fatima needed any help in the kitchen.

The call to prayer came from far away. They all got up to prepare themselves.

The men took their stand. Osama, Suad's husband, was the eldest so he took the lead. After him, the other men stood in a row and behind them came the women, who were wrapped in colourful garments that concealed everything but their faces. The boys stood next to the men and the girls next to the women.

"Why do the women stand in back? Are men standing in front because they are considered better?" Susie whispered to Ahmed.

"No", he said. "It is because a man's character is weak. It's difficult for a man to concentrate on praying when he sees a woman in front of him bowing down and standing up. Women don't care about standing behind the men because their characters are stronger."

At night, all the guests left the apartment to return home, leaving Fatima, Samia, Susie, and Ahmed. Fatima was happy to finally be living with her son under the same roof, and because Samia was not married, it was natural for her to stay with her brother and his wife.

Because Samia had become almost totally deaf following her

childhood illness, as a result her speech was blurred, and most people couldn't understand her. This made her shy in front of strangers, and so she avoided them, spending her time at home with her mother and her sisters when they came for a visit. She rarely left the house.

There were no schools for girls when Samia was growing up in Mecca, let alone schools for handicapped children. But Fatima was convinced that her daughter was not mentally retarded, as many people had told her because to them Samia's speech was unintelligible. It was just that small children replicate what they hear; since Samia couldn't perceive all sounds, she was unable to repeat them correctly. And so by not hearing, to a great extent her surroundings didn't make sense to her.

Fatima developed her own sign language that she used to communicate with Samia. As long as Samia's father was alive, he would have tried the impossible to help Samia. He even took her to Cairo because an Egyptian doctor in Mecca had told him about a specialist there. But even in the capital of Egypt they couldn't help Samia.

When Samia's sisters entered a newly opened school, Fatima insisted that Samia, too, should learn to read and write. Samia would sit next to her sisters while they were doing their homework. Suad would draw a house, then write the word *house* in Arabic, pronouncing slowly and clearly so that Samia could repeat. But this method of learning was very limited because Fatima and her daughters weren't fluent in reading and writing themselves.

When Ahmed went to study in Germany, he brought a hearing device home during one of his vacations. The cracking sounds Samia heard irritated her and made it difficult for others to deal with her. Over time, Samia learnt to make more use of the hearing aid, although she never really felt comfortable with it, and Fatima always had to remind her to use it.

Suad got married and moved to Riyadh, where her husband worked as a civil servant. They convinced Fatima to come with them. The first school for handicapped girls had been opened in Riyadh. Fatima asked Suad's husband to inquire about admission for Samia, but he was turned down on the grounds that Samia had become too old to enroll in the school.

Mornings, Ahmed went to work and Susie stayed home with Fatima and Samia. Fatima looked after her. She took her into the kitchen and talked to her, explaining in Arabic what she was doing. Slowly, Susie became accustomed to the sounds of the language, and she began understanding some of the constantly repeated words.

Fatima pointed to a pot and said:"Halla, halla."
She encouraged Susie to repeat: "halla, halla."
Susie tried: "hala."
Fatima smiled: "halla."
Susie tried again: "halla."
Fatima smiled happily. Next, she took an onion and said, "Basal."
Susie laughed: "Basal – that's easy."
Then Fatima pointed at the garlic: "toom."
And Susie repeated: "toom, toom."

Susie then wrote down all the new words she had learnt phonetically in the Latin alphabet, the way she heard them, and their meanings.

On the first day, Fatima taught Susie how to prepare *molokhia*, Ahmed's favourite dish.

In front of them, spread out on the table, were bunches of green twigs with small leaves. They picked the leaves, washed them, and put them on a cotton tablecloth to dry. Afterwards, the leaves were chopped until they formed a pappy green substance that smelled like grass. In the meantime, Fatima had boiled chicken, to which she added the green pap. Next, garlic and dried cilantro seeds were fried in ghee and added to the green soup.

Fatima explained to Susie that every step was very important for the correct taste, and that the recipe had been handed down to her by her mother, the same way she had taught her daughters.

Once Ahmed came home from work, lunch was served, and afterwards they would nap.

When they got up, they had tea; at night they would go out to visit one of Fatima's brothers and his family. On other days, they stayed home to receive the relatives who came to visit Fatima.

Ahmed had already explained to Susie that hospitality is very important in Arab society. It was part of hospitality that no guest should be offended or should leave the house of his host in a state of anger. A guest was always welcomed with an offer of juice, Arabic coffee, and dates, followed by tea, if it wasn't time for a meal.

Susie learnt how to prepare Arabic coffee and to greet people when they came to their house. She learnt how to cook *kabsa*, the traditional Arabic rice dish; to put on the *abaya*, the loose black robe that covers a woman from head to toe, when she left the house; and she learnt how to walk in long skirts. She got used to the heat and to the fact that the tap water was so hot in summer one had to be careful not to get scalded.

But sometimes, when she was standing at the window looking out, she thought about other women who lived in Riyadh. What were their lives like? Did they live the same way she did? Was there something else for women to do except cooking, cleaning, and visiting? What did other young women feel? How did they live their lives?

3.

"Today, you're invited to a wedding party", Ahmed told her one day after he came home from work.

"Me? Why just me – why not 'we'?" asked Susie.

"Because here, wedding parties are celebrated separately, men on their own and women among themselves. Zainab is also invited, so you can go with her."

"What should I wear? What do women here wear at a wedding party?"

"I don't know. Zainab will help you."

That night, Susie went with Ahmed to Zainab's house. She had on her best dress, the one she had bought in Germany the year before when she attended the wedding party of a colleague. She didn't have a lot of jewellery. Over the dress, she wore her abaya, which she always wore when they left the house.

Zainab looked at her.

"No, you can't go like this."

Zainab opened her closet and went through her dresses. Then she said in her best school English, "Your dress is not fancy enough, and you need to wear jewellery. All the women at the party know that Ahmed's wife has arrived; Riyadh is a small place, and gossip travels fast. Everybody will look at you, and they'll come to greet you. If you're not dressed properly, they'll blame me. Maybe I'll find something for you. We are almost the same size."

"Why can't I go the way I am?"

"If you go like that, people will think that Ahmed doesn't have enough money to buy a new dress for his wife. This will also reflect on us, his sisters."

"But that's true. We're just beginning to build a life for ourselves. We don't have much money for dresses and jewellery."

"But the women we'll see at the party don't think like that. They will say 'Why does he get married if he can't support his wife properly?' Here, people look at it superficially; they look at what you wear what car you're driving. If you have money, you must be important, so then people come to meet you. And it's important to know the right people."

Zainab helped Susie find a proper dress, apply make-up, fix her hair, and then loaned her a beautiful diamond necklace with matching earrings. Finally, she offered Susie one of her own extravagant, expensive abayas. When everything was ready, Zainab looked at Susie.

"Yes, now you look good. You'll make a good impression. Everybody will envy Ahmed."

At 10 p.m., they left for the party.

Zainab's driver took them to one of the five-star hotels. He stopped in front of a bright entrance at the side of the hotel, where they got out of the car. Susie couldn't see much, since Zainab had advised her to cover her face with a veil because of her make-up. Zainab gave the two invitation tickets to the man at the front door before they entered the hotel.

The doors were covered by heavy curtains.

Inside, Zainab and Susie removed their veils and abayas and handed them to the woman in the cloakroom. In return, they received a number.

As Susie entered the hall, she didn't know where to look. The spacious marble entrance opened onto a large lobby, in the middle of which was a big table with a huge flower arrangement. There were mirrors everywhere. Some women dressed in the latest fashions were standing in front of them fixing their hair and make-up.

"Zainab, what should I do? How do I behave?"

"It's not that difficult, don't panic. Follow me and do whatever I do. If somebody says something, say '*mabruk*'; that means 'congratulations'; you say '*forsa saida*', that means 'happy opportunity'."

Susie followed Zainab into the main hall where the party was taking place.

Some female relatives of the bride and the mother and sisters of the groom were standing at the door. Zainab and Susie greeted and kissed them according to the tradition of the western province of Saudi Arabia: one on the right cheek and then three kisses on the other. Susie said "*mabruk*", and from time to time, "*forsa saida*."

Zainab saw some of her friends, so she and Susie joined them at their table after they had greeted and kissed one another.

The tables and chairs in the main hall were arranged in such a way that the guests faced the right side of the hall, where a kind of stage had been built. On this stage was the *cosha*, the place for the bride and the groom. The theme of the cosha was a magic garden. Everything was bathed in light yellow. There were two armchairs for the couple to sit on and a small chest in between, with the gifts from the groom to his bride. Lots of yellow roses as well as white flowers were distributed everywhere on the *cosha*. On its left side were the seats for the all-female band.

One of Zainab's friends asked Susie something in Arabic, but just at that moment the band started to play. It was an Arabic song from the Gulf region, which the singer performed accompanied by her drum-beating friends. Susie felt like she was sitting in a nightclub. The music was much too loud for her, but it seemed that the other women enjoyed it. Many of them got up and danced. A young girl, perhaps sixteen, started to dance like she had seen in a video, her flexible movements striking. The other women stopped dancing, formed a circle around her, and clapped their hands to the rhythm of the music to encourage the girl.

Women in uniform walked around and offered the guests juice, water, coffee, and chocolates.

At that point, Susie felt that the noise and the loud music were getting to be a bit too much, so she got up and walked out of the hall to take a break.

"Aren't you Susie, the wife of Ahmed? I know your sisters-in-law; my name is Reham."

Susie turned around. A young, beautiful woman with black hair and black eyes was standing in front of her. She spoke to Susie in English.

"Hi, Reham. I'm happy to meet you."

"Is this your first wedding party in Riyadh?"

"Yes. I've never seen a Saudi wedding before. It's all a little bit strange for me. Do you know the bride?"

"No, the groom is a cousin of mine."

"How did the couple meet?"

"They didn't actually meet, their marriage was arranged. My cousin wanted to get married. He'd just graduated from college and had found a good job, so he told his mother and his sisters that they should look for a wife for him."

"Any wife?" asked Susie, not sure if she should believe her.

"No, he described the woman he was looking for. He wanted her to be a few years younger than himself; she should be pretty and have a good personality. He told them it was important for him that his future wife should get along well with his family. As soon as he described her, his sister Iman thought about her friend. So Iman and her mother went to meet the future bride and her mother. Iman's mother liked the girl, so they talked to my cousin, and then my cousin and his father went to meet the father of the bride. After that, when everything was arranged and everybody was satisfied, my cousin went to their house to meet the girl. And he liked her."

"But that means they don't know each other. They don't know anything about the other."

"Yes, but this is our tradition. This is the way we are brought up. We don't want anything else. This works for us. And our marriages are no better or worse than those in the Western world. I think, for some people, this is an easier system; others prefer the Western way. It all has its advantages and disadvantages. In Saudi Arabia, many girls get married to men of their own extended family, so they more or less know each other before they get married."

"It's so loud inside. Is it always this loud?"

Reham laughed. "You've got to learn to dance. When you move your body to the music, you'll enjoy even loud music. Come, I'll show you."

Susie followed Reham back inside the wedding hall. She looked at the dancing women and tried to imitate them. Soon she realised that she was actually enjoying herself, so that even the loud music no longer bothered her. Some of the other dancing women smiled when they saw Susie and how she tried to imitate them. One of them positioned herself in front of Susie and through her movements tried to encourage her. She moved her hips, clapped her hands, looked at Susie and said, "*Yella*, let's dance."

Suddenly the music stopped. The dancers hastily returned to their seats.
"The bride is coming."
Immediately everybody sat down. Some of the women covered themselves up with their abayas.
Through the loudspeakers now came the sound of romantic Western music. Spotlights positioned opposite the *cosha* lit up the entrance. A little girl in a long, light-yellow dress entered the room, scattering flowers on the floor as she walked. A small boy in a long white gown, called a *thob*, followed her. He was wearing a white cloth, a *ghutra*, on his head and tried not to move his hands so the Quran he was carrying on a cushion wouldn't fall off. Behind him came an older girl who whispered instructions to the little boy. The girl was also dressed in light yellow and was carrying a lighted yellow candle.
Then the bride entered with the groom. They moved slowly, walking in time to the music. The bride wore a beautiful long white dress and carried a bouquet of yellow roses. Her face was covered by a white veil. The groom wore a white *thob*, covered by a black *mishlah*, and a white *ghutra*. Neither the bride nor her groom looked at each other. When they arrived at the *cosha*, they sat down. Their mothers rushed by to help them. The mother of the bride lifted her daughter's veil, while the mother of the groom took a diamond necklace from the gift chest. She helped her son place it around his bride's neck.

The guests who were closest to the *cosha* could see that his hands were shaking. The mothers looked at each other and smiled.

The band started playing once again. The sisters of the bride and the groom and their mothers then danced in front of the newlyweds. A female photographer took pictures of the couple – first just the two of them, then with the sisters, with the mothers, and then with anyone else who wanted to be in the picture.

Some women in uniform wheeled in the wedding cake. The married couple got up to cut the cake together. They tried to feed each other a mouthful of the cake. It wasn't easy. The bride's hand shook; the groom took her hand in his.

Then the bride and the groom exited the hall, her arm in his as they whispered to each other, the bride smiling happily as they left the hall.

The women who had donned their abayas then uncovered themselves and everyone got up.

"Come, the buffet is open", Zainab said. Susie followed her to an adjacent room.

Tables seating eight had been prepared for the guests. Zainab and Susie looked for an empty table, put their purses on it, and went to get some food. The buffet was arranged along two walls. At the beginning of the line were plates, napkins, and flatware, followed by different kinds of salads and hors d'oeuvres. Then there were three huge plates with whole cooked lambs and rice. In-between were serving dishes with lasagna, different kinds of vegetables, roast beef, potatoes, grilled chicken, different kinds of grilled and baked fish, and scampi.

At the other end of the room was a table covered with desserts: chocolate mousse, fancy cakes, crème caramel, and a lot of different kinds of fruit.

"What time is it?"

"We've got to go", Zainab said. "Are you ready? It's 3:30 in the morning; soon they'll call for the morning prayer."

Outside, Ahmed was already waiting for them. They had agreed that he would pick them up because he didn't want Susie and Zainab to be out in the streets at night with the driver. As soon as they were seated in the car, the muezzin began to call for prayer. From all directions it came: "*Allahu Akbar, Allahu Akbar, ashhadu an la ilaha il Allah.*"

4.

Reham woke up when she heard the baby. It was still dark outside. She got up quickly so her sleeping husband would not awaken. If his sleep was disturbed, Bandar would be grouchy all day and would ask her again to move the baby bed to another room. Reham took Dahlia out of her crib and went to the other room. She changed her diapers before breastfeeding. It was always the same: as soon as she looked at her daughter, her sleep was gone; she only wanted to hold her. She loved this time of the day, when the house was quiet and there was only her daughter and herself.

"I want you to be happy", she whispered in the baby's tiny ears.

She had hardly got back to bed when the voice of her husband woke her up again.

"I've got to go to work, where's my breakfast?"

Reham got up, checked on the sleeping baby, and then went downstairs to prepare breakfast.

Her mother-in-law's maid was already there. She had set the table, and after Reham fried some eggs and heated up some beans, the maid went upstairs to call mother and son. Reham prepared tea for the three of them.

After breakfast, Bandar left for work, and Reham went back upstairs to her rooms. She would see her mother-in-law again only when it was time to cook lunch.

In the afternoon, after her husband had taken his nap, she went to have tea with him.

"Can I please talk to you?" she asked.

Bandar seemed to be in one of his better moods.

"What's bothering you today?"

"I want to work. You know that I love Dahlia, but I have so much spare time and I want to do something useful."

"There is nothing more useful in a woman's life than to raise children."

"Yes, you are right. But when you came to my father's house to marry me, I told you that as soon as I finished my studies I wanted to work, and you agreed."

"Yes, that's what I said then. But things have changed. You are a mother now, and a mother must look after her children."

"Your mother is at home all day long, and she has her maid to help her. She loves Dahlia – she could look after her."

"I don't want you to work. I want you to stay in the house and take care of me and of Dahlia."

Reham knew that to continue to try to discuss the matter with him would be useless. She loved her daughter dearly, but she felt as though she was suffocating. She didn't like spending her time with her mother-in-law watching sitcoms on TV all day long and listening to her complain about the maid. Her mother-in-law had been a widow for many years; she was very close to Bandar, her eldest son. One of Reham's problems was that she didn't want to adapt to their way of life. There was also an age difference: Bandar was fifteen years older than Reham, and they had different goals in life. Bandar wanted to have a good, comfortable life and raise his children. He always talked about being "respectable". He despised changes and believed that life was good just as it was. Reham wanted to have a family, but she also craved a life of her own; her goal was not simply to be the mother of Dahlia or the wife of Bandar; she also wanted to be Reham: she wanted a career.

The next day, she decided to talk to her mother-in-law; maybe she would understand her feelings. To get off to a good start, she went downstairs when she knew Bandar's mother was watching one of her Egyptian sitcoms. Reham made some tea and took the tray to her. But once again Reham had forgotten to add mint leaves, and the tea was too weak for her mother-in-law's taste. Reluctantly, she decided to postpone her talk to a later time.

She went back upstairs to check on Dahlia, who was still sleeping, so she just sat there. Reham was depressed; she was unhappy and didn't have the strength to get herself out of it. As long as she could remember, all she ever wanted was to study and work; she never thought about marriage. Her mother thought her wishes inappropriate for a young Saudi girl and made every effort to persuade her that only married life would give her fulfillment. When Bandar first came to the house, her parents were more than happy to make wedding arrangements. Reham tried to talk to her mother about their age difference, but her mother dismissed her objections. She said that Bandar was a man in his best years; he had settled down, had experience, and because he was also prosperous he would take good care of his wife. Reham told her that she was not attracted to him; her mother replied that affection was not important. Money and prestige were what a girl should look for in a husband.

Reham had listened to her mother and now here she was, in this big house with her husband and his mother, feeling alienated, lonely.

When she knew that her mother-in-law was preparing lunch, Reham again went down to the kitchen. She made an effort to help, but Bandar's mother didn't like the way she cut the vegetables.

"I think I can never please you or your son", Reham said.

"We're very easy to please, but you always think that you're so much better. If only you'd do as we tell you, you'd be happy."

Reham tried to explain to her that she was unhappy staying at home; she wanted to work.

"In our family, we don't have wives leaving their husbands' houses. What would people think if you worked? I won't agree to this, and if Bandar asks me, I'll tell him so."

Reham felt it was of no use; she mumbled something about hearing the baby crying and went upstairs to her room.

She looked at the sleeping infant. She was such a beautiful little girl. But was it enough for this child to have a mother who was always unhappy and depressed? Wouldn't it be much better for her to grow up in a happy environment? Dahlia loved her grandmother and her daddy; Reham felt they both had the experience and know-how to bring up a child – unlike herself, who was too ambitious to be a stay-at-home mother. If things continued this way, maybe Dahlia might become unhappy, too, she thought.

Reham put her head on the crib and couldn't keep from sobbing.

5.

The house was quiet. Fatima and Samia had wanted to visit Suad, so Ahmed gave them a ride. He, too, wanted to see his sister. Susie didn't feel like going out or sitting with the family. While they would laugh and joke, she wouldn't be able to understand what it was all about. Instead, she decided to stay home and write the letter she had been planning to write for weeks.

Dear Gitta,

I cannot tell you in words how much I miss you! You are my dearest friend.

Remember, before I left Germany, how you made me promise to tell you all about my "adventure", as you called it? I know that you are worried about me. But ever since I met Ahmed, he has been my life, and I would follow him anywhere.

As you know, we decided to travel to Saudi Arabia by car because it was less expensive, we were able to take all our belongings with us in the trunk, and I thought it would be easier for me to leave Germany and come to the Middle East gradually, not by getting into a plane in Frankfurt and getting off in Riyadh. This way I saw Turkey, Syria, and Jordan and was able to get prepared for what life in the Middle East is like.

By the way, I loved the journey, sitting in the car next to Ahmed and being close to him. I remember the evenings in Syria, when in the twilight we could hear the crickets chirping. It was so peaceful, and I thought to myself that all I'm leaving behind, do I really need it? Isn't what I have enough to make me happy?

We arrived in Riyadh in the early morning hours. The city looked peaceful at that time of day even though we didn't hear any crickets or see many trees. But we are in the middle of the desert, so what can one expect?

Ahmed's mother opened the door for us as we arrived. She is such a nice woman. She immediately reminded me of my own mother. She has a similar build, with the same kind, fine, amicable expression in her face.

But, to tell you the truth, the rest of the family doesn't seem to be too thrilled about my presence. They try to be nice because they don't want to upset their brother. Ahmed's oldest sister is shy because she doesn't hear well. Even though we live in the same apartment, she and I don't interact that much. She knows I'm here, but she ignores me more or less.

Zainab, his other sister, is different. She's the boss in the family, she tells everybody what to do. I think she doesn't want me here. You know, my Arabic is not good, but I understand a lot better than I can speak. I overheard them one day saying that Zainab had already found a wife for Ahmed before I came along. Her husband speaks German and also has some books that he offered to lend me. But I don't want to make a fuss in the family or cause any offence, so I think it's better not to take him up on his offer, despite the fact that there are no German books available here. Zainab's husband said he bought the books abroad. Maybe it's not good if I talk to him too often, somebody could get a different idea. Zainab loves her brother very much, so right now she accepts me because I belong to him. However, if I do it right, maybe one day I'll get her to love me, too. Ahmed's sister Suad is okay; she's polite, I think she doesn't want to get into a disagreement with Zainab over me.

The sisters endure my existence, waiting to see what will happen. They never try to talk to me on their own, not like their mother. I feel that she loves me because I'm me, not because I'm her son's wife.

What else can I tell you? I'm learning Arabic, which is very difficult. There are so many sounds I cannot make. And I'm learning cooking and cleaning the Arab way.

I want so much to make this work. I want to be part of the family, and if that means I have to act like a Saudi woman, I'm prepared to give up everything.

Your friend,
Susie

6.

"Today I met a colleague of mine who works with a German, and he told my colleague that the German women here meet once a month in the morning", Ahmed told Susie when he came home. "Do you want to go? I could give you a ride, and when you're finished, I'd pick you up. They meet in a hotel for breakfast."

The following Monday, on the day the women got together, Susie woke up very early. She was excited. She'd have an opportunity to speak German. She'd be able to understand every word they were saying, not just the general meaning of what somebody said. And she wouldn't feel out of place as she mostly did when everybody around her spoke Arabic.

She put on her "German" clothes – her favourite jeans and a t-shirt. Over it, she put on her abaya.

When they arrived at the hotel, Ahmed accompanied her inside. The hotel employees immediately took care of her and told her where to go. Susie said good-bye to Ahmed and entered the adjoining hall.

Inside, there were nine tables with chairs. The right side of the hall had huge windows that were covered with heavy white curtains so that nobody from the outside garden would be able to look inside. Some artificial trees had been placed around in the corners; they looked almost real. On each table stood a small vase with some silk flowers.

A few women were sitting at different tables. Susie approached the table closest to her and asked if she could have a seat, but the woman at the table told her that she was still waiting for her friends and that all the seats were taken. Susie looked around. A few tables away, two middle-aged women were sitting and talking. When they noticed Susie, they smiled at her. Susie went to them and greeted them in German. One of them replied: "Good morning. My name is Ingrid, this is Jutta. Come, sit with us." Then they continued talking to one another.

Soon, other women arrived and took the seats their friends had reserved for them. Everyone was greeted with a big "hello", and soon small groups formed.

"How was your vacation? When did you come back? Show me, is that a new dress? It looks great."

"Look, I have a new bracelet. I bought it yesterday."

"Where did you get it? I want to get a new necklace. Really, nowhere is gold as cheap as it is here."

"Did you go to the new mall? It's very nice, all the great fashion houses. You really have to go there. You won't find anything better in Germany, and even the prices are less expensive."

"We got a new car. The old one didn't look that good any more. My husband wanted a Lexus, but I convinced him to buy a new Mercedes."

"Did you move into your new house? Are you going to buy the furniture here or from Germany?"

Susie felt dizzy just listening. She looked at the woman who had just come in and taken the seat next to her. She seemed to be her age. Susie introduced herself.

"Hi. My name is Susie. I'm new here."

"Hi, Susie, I'm Almud. How do you feel living in Riyadh? Why did you come here?"

"My husband is Saudi. He just finished his studies in Germany, and so here we are."

"My husband is working here; he's German. There is Eva; her

husband is Saudi, too. Eva", she called over to a woman who seemed about their age, "this is Susie; she's new."

Because the seat next to Eva was not occupied, Susie moved over.

"Good morning. Is your name really Susie? Are you as green and naïve as your name implies in German?" Eva joked.

"I like my name! My husband says the name fits me. I don't understand why I always have to defend it", she said. Then she asked, "How long have you lived here?"

"Five long years", Eva replied.

"You don't like Riyadh?"

"I can't say that I don't like it, we have a good life, but this is not Germany. My husband, who's Saudi, is a physician, he works too much, and I don't see him that often. Most of the time I'm alone with the kids."

"What about his family? Don't they come to visit you?"

"I don't understand most of the things they tell me. Usually my husband visits them alone. Sometimes he takes the kids. My mother-in-law doesn't like me. She wanted a Saudi wife for her son. Where do you live?"

"We live in Olaya. My mother-in-law lives with us and one of my sisters-in-law."

"What? You agreed to live with them? I could never do that."

"My mother-in-law is old", Susie said. "She only has one son, my husband. She loves him very much, and she's so happy that we live together. Do you speak Arabic well?"

"No, and I don't want to learn it. Why should I? Whoever wants to talk to me can talk to me in German or in English."

"Don't listen to Eva", Ingrid interrupted. "She's not very happy here. I think if her husband's family had welcomed her, Eva's attitude would be different. She's afraid that her mother-in-law will push her aside and marry Eva's husband off to a Saudi, and then Eva would have to share her husband with another woman."

"No, it's not only that", said Eva. "My husband is very weak in front of his mother; he thinks that out of respect he has to obey her. When we visit his family together, he always feels overpowered by one or the other of us and doesn't know what to do, whether he should listen to me or to his mother. And his mother always tries to manipulate her children."

Susie turned to Ingrid: "How long have you lived here? Do you speak Arabic?"

"I've been living in Riyadh for more than twenty years. I like it here. I have many friends, Arabs and foreigners, some of them are Muslims and some are Christians. We all respect one another. Here I have the opportunity to meet people from different cultures; there are so many people from all over the world. If you like, you can come with me the next time I visit one of my friends."

"We don't have a driver", Susie replied. "It's difficult for me to get around. My husband doesn't like it if I take a taxi, and as you know, there is no public transportation here for women."

"That's true, you can't take a bus. And I wouldn't take a taxi on my own, either", Ingrid said. "When I was new in Riyadh, I once took a taxi. At that time I was working in a hospital and my husband wasn't in Riyadh to give me a ride. The taxi driver took me into the desert. At first I wondered why he took a different route, but he told me that he was taking a shortcut. When I realised where I was, I started to shout at him in Arabic. I don't know where the words came from! I used all the dirty words I had ever heard. It was probably the shock that I talked to him in Arabic in such a way that he immediately drove me to the hospital by the shortest route."

"What is the biggest problem you have here?" Susie asked.

"For me, the biggest problems are the things that concern my children", the woman next to them said.

"Why, Jutta?" Almud asked.

"My husband is Saudi and so are my kids. As Saudis, they are supposed to go to Saudi schools. But my Arabic is not good enough to help them with their schoolwork. We could hire a private teacher to help them, but right now we don't have the money. Last year, my daughter had problems with algebra. During my last year in high school, one of the subjects I specialised in was mathematics, so I thought I could study with her", Jutta sighed. "Every day, after school, we sat together and I practised with her. It wasn't as easy as I thought because, as you know, they use different numerals here. But the result was that my daughter got into even more trouble because I use a different method than what her teacher uses, and in the end my daughter was totally confused. I wanted to go to the school to talk to the teacher, but most of the teachers don't speak that much English or German so I couldn't talk to them. And my husband can't go to school because men are prohibited from entering girls' schools. And none of the teachers has agreed to talk to my husband on the phone."

"Yah, that's true", Ingrid agreed. "Homework is a problem. We solved the problem when my husband studied with my first-born daughter, and when she was old enough, she taught her sisters and her brother. But I felt so useless, not even schoolwork could I help them with; I felt illiterate."

"And what are the other problems?" Susie inquired.

"Our children have a special place in this society. They're not really accepted as Saudis, but they also don't belong to the groups of foreigners; they are in-between", Ingrid told her. "That should be positive because they know both worlds, the Western and the Arabic. But I think they'll only see the advantage of that when they're older."

"But except for that, our life is more or less normal", Ingrid continued. "I mean, we can't drive a car, but one gets accustomed to that. I think it's great that somebody drives me; I don't have to drive myself. I don't need to carry grocery bags, and I don't need to look for a parking space. It's not that bad!"

"What do you like about Riyadh?" Susie asked her.

"Really, there are some positive aspects. You know, Susie, my husband is Saudi", said Ingrid. "This is his culture and the culture of my children, who grew up and went to school here. If I don't participate in their Islamic way of life, parts of their lives are closed to me. And I think any culture I learn about enriches my own life. Many things we notice in other people we think they don't make sense, that the people are backwards; but when we know more about the culture, we begin to understand why things are the way they are. We have to look beyond, and we should always ask, 'Why?'"

"This is all nonsense", Eva interrupted. "To ask 'Why?' and to read your history lessons, that's old stuff. We are living today, and we live here, and here everything is complicated. I don't understand it, and I don't want to understand."

"And what about your kids, Eva?" Susie wanted to know.

"They have to find their own way, as I had to find mine. My husband has married a German; I was German when we met and I will stay a German, the way I was."

"Ladies, stop it", Almud said impatiently. "Come, let's go to the buffet. I'm hungry."

At the buffet, Susie stood next to an older woman.
"What's this?" she asked, pointing at one of the dishes.
"Those are sambosaks. You're new in Riyadh?"
"Yes, I just arrived a few months ago. My name is Susie."
"I'm Roswita; I've been living here a long time."
"Is your husband Saudi?"
"Yes, and I have adult children. My son got married last year and I'll be a grandmother soon."
"Oh, that means you're at home here."
"More or less. But often I feel as if I sit between two chairs – one part of my bottom sits on one chair and the other part on the other chair. I don't sit comfortably, but if I move over to the right chair, I don't feel at ease, the chair doesn't fit any more. Each chair is comfortable", Roswita explained jokingly, as she took a piece of bread and some cheese. "My bottom is accustomed to the in-between sitting, and when you sit uncomfortably for a long time, this is what your bottom knows. You don't like it any other way. The left chair also doesn't fit – it's not made for German bottoms. You try to sit comfortably, you try hard, but the chair always pinches you. It's too narrow. Some people like narrow chairs, they feel protected and guarded in them, but for me it's too tight. Sometimes I want to get up. I don't want to sit any more, not on the right chair and not on

the left chair, not even on the rift, in-between. But to look for a new chair, after all these years? This is what you bought; nobody forced the chairs on you, so you do your best to make the chair and the rift in-between fit as best as possible."

"That means you're not happy here?" Susie asked her.

"No, I wouldn't exactly say that. My family lives here, and for my children, this is home. Sometimes I get homesick, especially at Christmastime. But when I'm in Germany I get homesick for Riyadh. So you see, nothing is ideal for us any more", Roswita laughed. Then she continued:

"If you really look at it, this here, our coming together like this, makes us feel at home. Here I find women who are like me; we are family, sisters. Here we have more in common with one another than we do with our families in Germany."

Ingrid interrupted them: "Hey, the two of you, are you done? Come over here, we want to talk about our next meeting."

7.

The heavy iron gate closed with a loud clang. Susie looked around. High walls were behind her and in front of her. Some thirty metres away was a two-story building. Should she remove her face veil? It was hot under her abaya, which felt heavy on her head.

"*Enti min?*" she heard a voice.

Susie turned around. Behind her was a young woman dressed in a long black skirt and a white blouse with long sleeves.

"*Ana … ana Susie*", she tried to answer.

"Ah, that must mean you're the new English teacher", the woman said in English.

Susie was relieved. "Yes, where should I go?"

"I'll show you. My name is Mona. Don't you want to take off your abaya? I'll take you to meet *Abla* Hessa, the director of the school. Her name is Hessa, but we call her *Abla*, as a sign of respect."

"Yeah, thank you", Susie replied.

She removed her abaya and her face veil and rolled them together. Zainab had told her to put on a long black skirt and a white blouse. Thank God she'd listened to her.

She followed Mona into the building.

Inside, the walls were covered with huge paintings. One showed the desert and a few mud houses with flowers and palm trees. On the other wall was a painting with a river with trees and plants on its shores. The third wall had a painting showing a large hand that threw something in a garbage can; next to it was something written in Arabic.

In the middle of the school building was a huge yard, with the classrooms located around it. Most of the doors were open, and low voices could be heard.

Susie saw two girls in grey uniforms on the second floor. As soon as they noticed Mona and Susie, they stooped in order not to be seen by them.

Abla Hessa sat behind a large desk, talking on the telephone as they entered. She was a middle-aged, over-weight woman without make-up, dressed in a black skirt and a white, long-sleeved blouse. As soon as she finished her phone call, she looked at Susie, and Mona explained something to her in Arabic. *Abla* Hessa smiled at Susie, and then got up to greet her. She said something to Mona in Arabic but Susie didn't understand her.

"*Abla* Hessa says that you should come with me. I'll give you everything you need, and then I'll show you the two teachers' rooms and your desk. Come", Mona said to Susie.

Susie followed Mona to the upper floor. On the right side were two rooms full of teachers' desks. They entered the second room. In the middle of the room was a long table where six teachers were sitting. On the table were two thermoses of coffee, some small cups, and some dates. Mona introduced Susie to the other teachers. They looked at Susie in surprise. They were dressed in long skirts and blouses with long sleeves. One of the teachers pointed to an empty desk that Susie could use. Mona disappeared but returned after a few minutes with some books in her arms.

"These are the books you should use for your classes, this is your timetable, and this here is our Teachers' Book. In it you'll find exact instructions on how you should teach. But if you want, you can use your own method if you think it's better. That's what I do", Mona said. "Only when *Abla* Hessa or the inspector, *Abla* Maha, come to check on your teaching, it's better to follow the Teachers' Book. If you have any questions, come to me or ask *Abla* Nura, she sits here in the room, speaks English, and she, too, teaches the eleventh grade.

It's better that you start tomorrow with your lessons; as you probably know, the school year started three weeks ago, but your students didn't have a teacher for most of that time. Good luck to you!"

Susie sat down at her new desk and started preparing herself for the lessons. At least now she had something to do that was familiar and gave her some confidence.

Through Ahmed and his connections, Susie had found the job as an English teacher at one of the public girls' schools on the outskirts of Riyadh.

She had realised that she depended totally on Ahmed. He was her interpreter, he went shopping with her, he told her the latest news, he introduced her to people. There was no information that came to her without coming first to Ahmed. If Ahmed wasn't there, she didn't know what to do. It was Ahmed who told her how to behave "in a proper way" and what to say without leaving a bad impression on people. And if Ahmed couldn't be with her, like when she was sitting with women, Zainab was there to help.

Susie understood that she had to build her own life with a circle of friends who respected her and didn't look down on her because she wasn't Saudi. She needed to learn to behave in a Saudi environment without offending anybody. And even if she made a mistake, in this way she would be able to integrate into Saudi society and be accepted by people.

It was Zainab's idea that Susie should work again, as an English teacher, like she had in Germany. Zainab worked in another school and she knew there was always a demand for teachers. She encouraged Ahmed to find Susie a job in a school so that she would have an opportunity to become independent and learn more about the life of women in Saudi society. Susie wanted to work, but when Ahmed first told her that she could teach again, she was hesitant. She didn't know much Arabic; she had no idea about the school system. But what else would there be for her to do? Susie wanted so much to have a life of her own, away from Ahmed's family and their protective net, that she finally overcame her own worries and accepted the job.

The first day she was to teach at the school, Susie made sure she arrived on time. The bell rang as she entered the school, but strangely enough nobody seemed to care. The schoolyard was crowded with girls in their grey uniforms. Some of the girls looked at Susie curiously and started whispering as she passed by.

Abla Hessa came out of the school building with some of the teachers at her side. They clapped their hands and told the girls to line up.

Over the microphone came the voice of a girl reciting a verse from the Quran. When she was finished, the girls entered the school in pairs. *Abla* Hessa stood at the school door making sure the students were properly dressed in their uniforms, their hair pulled back, their fingernails trimmed short, and that they were wearing proper shoes, no flip-flops or sandals.

And Susie went to her first class.

As she was about to enter the classroom, Susie stopped at the door. She was shocked. Sitting in front of her were about fifty teenage girls in grey uniforms. All of them had chairs, but not all had desks. There was no way a teacher could pass through to get to the back of the class. The students were sitting so close together that some of them had to place their arms around the chairs of the girls next to them.

"Good morning", Susie said in English.
"Good morning", the girls answered in chorus.
"I'm your new teacher. My name is Susie."
"Where are you from?"
"I'm from Germany."
"Welcome to our school."
"How much English do you know? Where did you stop in the book?"

And so, Susie started her first lesson.

Sitting immediately in front of her were two girls who were eager to participate. They competed with each other in trying to be the first one to answer her questions.

Near the end of the period, Susie explained the homework. She left the classroom as soon as the bell rang. Outside the room, the next teacher, who had been waiting just outside the door, immediately entered the classroom.

Like this, Susie proceeded to her next four classes.

At noon, Ahmed was waiting outside the school to give her a ride home.

"It wasn't that bad, much easier than I expected", she told him as they drove home.

The next morning, as she was about to enter the classroom, Susie noticed there was some turmoil inside. The girls were standing in small groups, discussing and shouting.

"Good morning", Susie said.

Some of the girls looked at her and went to their seats. By and by, the other girls followed their example until after some time, they were all seated.

"Open your books. Read the paragraph on page fifteen and answer the questions."

Slowly, a few girls started opening their bags, took out their books, and looked around. Susie opened her book to page fifteen and showed the page to the girls. The students tried to find the page, and after they found it, they looked at the writing.

Susie tried to pass through the girls to the back of the room, to make sure they had all opened to the correct page, but she had to give up. There was just no easy way to get to the girls in the back.

After five minutes had passed, she asked, "What is the answer to question number one?"

The girls looked at her in bewilderment.

"What is your answer?" Susie asked a beautiful, slim girl with dark hair sitting in the last row.

The girl got up, looking at Susie.

Another girl in the front row put her hand up.

"Teacher, that's Hanan. She doesn't understand you. She doesn't know what you've asked her. She doesn't know English."

"Then who understands the question?"

Two girls in the front row put up their hands.

"We answered all the questions."

"What about the other girls?" Susie asked them.

"They don't know how to read. They didn't understand the exercise."

"That means that all we did yesterday, they didn't understand it?"

"Only Wafa and myself. My name is Kholoud. The other girls don't like English. They don't understand it."

"Why not?"

Kholoud was short with long curly hair pulled back in a French twist. She looked older than her age. She turned around and talked to the other students in Arabic. Immediately, everybody started talking and answering in Arabic.

"Hanan, why don't you like English?" Susie asked.

Kholoud turned to Hanan and interpreted in Arabic.

"Teacher, she says that she only likes Arabic. She's Muslim. Arabic is the language of paradise. Arabic is the language of the Holy Quran. She says she doesn't know one reason why she should learn English."

"And the other girls, what do they say?"

"Most of the girls think the same way. And most of them think that Arabic is an easy language. They think that English is a very difficult language to learn."

"But Kholoud, there is a saying of the Prophet that it is the duty of every Muslim to acquire new knowledge."

"Teacher, are you a Muslim? You don't even know Arabic. But for us, every day we learn new things about our religion. Why do we need knowledge that comes from nonbelievers?"

"Okay, that means that you're all satisfied with the way the nonbelievers divided the world and the Islamic lands?"

"Some of us are not interested in this life. We are interested in the life that comes after. Then we go to paradise if we didn't sin. However some others only want to have fun."

"So you think it's better to put your head in the sand and let others dictate your life, or even let them impose their life on you because you don't want to know about the outside world?"

"No, *in sha Allah*, never. But other people are responsible for what will happen. We are weak, we can't do anything."

"You see, Kholoud, I believe that everybody has a task in life", Susie explained. "If we don't fulfil this task because we're lazy or we would rather do something easier, then that will have consequences later. If everybody did her job well, I think the world would be a better place."

"But that's difficult. We want to have some fun now."

"Yes, we should have some fun; but to reach our goals and to live our lives well, we have to contribute. Nothing comes without hard work. I feel that it is my task to teach you and open your eyes to other possibilities. I want to tell you about the Western world and the people there, who are not so much different from you. And I want to learn from you, too, so that I can understand your lives better."

The whole time, Kholoud had been translating to the other students what Susie had said. When she finished, some of the students showed their agreement in gestures and words.

"Teacher, I've an idea", Wafa said. "You teach us English and we teach you Arabic. Then we can all talk to one another."

"That's a good idea", Susie replied. "But let that be a secret between us, or the other classes will ridicule us. And imagine what the teachers will say. They'd be shocked!"

The next morning, Susie entered the classroom.

"Good morning."

Kholoud put up her hand. "Teacher, we are Muslims. You don't enter a room and say 'good morning'. That's not good. Why don't you say *Salam alaikum*?"

"But you should learn English!" Susie thought for a moment. "Okay, first I'll say '*Salam alaikum*', and then I'll say 'Good morning'. What do you think?"

They all agreed to this, and so Susie started the day's lesson.

The next day, Wafa was absent.

"Where is Wafa? Is she sick?" Susie asked Kholoud.

"No, she's getting married next week, and there are too many preparations."

"Why does she get married now? I thought she liked school."

"She does. But this young man came to Wafa's father and asked for her hand. Her father likes the man. He says he is a good Muslim, and so he gave him his permission. The young man agreed that Wafa can finish her schooling."

"Then let us start."

Susie looked around. Several other students whose names she didn't know were not in the classroom.

"Where are the other girls? Why aren't they here?"

Again Kholoud explained: "During the break, there was a religious lecture in the prayer room. They discussed how girls can become better Muslims. *Abla* Abrar is organizing such a meeting once every week. The students are encouraged to talk about their problems. They haven't come back yet. You came early. Do you want me to go get them?"

"Yes, please, Kholoud."

As Susie was about to go into her next class, she heard the loud voices of the students inside the room. Even as she entered, the room didn't quiet down.

"Why are you making so much noise? What has happened?"

"We just finished our test in psychology. And the test was so difficult! We cannot learn English now! We can't concentrate."

"Okay, I understand how you feel. So what do you want to do?"

"Today let's sit and talk, have some fun."

"But what are we going to do with the material we're supposed to cover today?" asked Susie.

"We'll do it tomorrow."

"And the material for tomorrow?"

The students looked at one another disappointed, but one of them suggested, "Why don't you come to us when we are free, like tomorrow, in the sixth period, we have no lesson then. Oh, please. Let us just sit and talk together now. Give us a break! We've studied all night long. We didn't sleep. Now we're really exhausted. Teacher, look at my eyes. I can't even keep them open."

"Okay, you can have the period off", Susie laughed. "But when I come back, you have to concentrate and work with me, or …"

"We will, we will. We'll do everything you want us to do! Tomorrow, tomorrow, we'll do it all."

The next day, *Abla* Hessa entered the classroom as Susie was about to correct the students' homework. *Abla* Hessa looked around.

"Who's absent?" she asked.

The students didn't answer. Susie looked at Kholoud, but Kholoud avoided her gaze.

"In the back, in the last row, there are three students missing", Susie replied.

"They've been absent the whole day?" *Abla* Hessa asked.

"Who's the class leader?"

Kholoud got up. "The girls Haifa, Hajer, and Gamra are in school, but they didn't come back after the break."

"That's what I thought", *Abla* Hessa said. "Somebody heard voices in the restrooms and I suspected that it was their voices."

She turned to Susie. "I want to talk to you outside."

Outside the classroom, she said to Susie, "Didn't you notice that the girls were not there? Why didn't you tell the administration about it?"

"I thought they were absent."

"Why didn't you check to see if their bags were there or not? Don't let the girls abuse you. You always have to show them who the stronger one is. The girls say that you're too nice to them. For them, that's a weakness."

"But the girls don't like English. I only try to motivate them. I don't think I can get their attention by force. I think that if I'm nice to them, they'll like my subject, and sooner or later they'll work with me."

"I heard complaints about you. Some teachers say that your students are always noisy."

"I know", Susie replied. "I noticed that, too. When I pass by other classrooms, there are hardly any noises, much less noise than in my classes. I don't know what I do wrong."

"Tomorrow when you enter your class, first take out the notebook where you write down the students' marks", *Abla* Hessa advised her. "Every girl who didn't do her homework gets a minus; those who talk get a minus; those who don't know how to read get a minus. And then, threaten them – tell them that if they don't participate or aren't polite, you'll make the next test really difficult, so difficult that they won't be able to answer and then they'll fail English, so that they'll have to repeat the school year. You'll see, a few days like that and the students will all sit like soldiers."

As the period came to a close, Susie felt very tired – exhausted and frustrated. She went to the teachers' room and put her head on her desk.

She heard a noise and when she looked up, one of the teachers stood in front of her desk. She was around Susie's age, tall and had her long, black hair pulled back into a pony tail.

"Are you not feeling well? You look tired", she said to Susie in English.

Susie looked at her, wondering who she was.

"Oh, I didn't introduce myself. I'm Latifa. I also teach English, but I was absent for some time. I just came to see you."

"Hi, Latifa. I don't know what's wrong. Everything is so different. Everything is so complicated. I have the feeling that I am doing it all wrong."

"Why, what happened?"

Susie told her about her encounter with *Abla* Hessa.

"Oh, don't worry", Latifa said, trying to reassure her. "Those are the girls of the literary section. Here, in this part of Riyadh, the girls are not really motivated to learn. It's true, they want to get out of this neighbourhood, but they know that they don't really have a chance to get into university; their marks are not good enough. And what can a Saudi girl with a secondary-school certificate do?

They can go for two years to one of the private institutes, but these cost money and most fathers here are not willing to pay for their daughters' education. The girls don't really have many possibilities except marriage, and they know it."

Latifa smiled and continued: "I've already heard so much about you. We all admire you and think it's great that you, a European, want to share our lives. There isn't a day we don't feel frustrated. You don't realise how much your presence means to us. Take it easy. Welcome to our life."

8.

Slowly, Susie began to learn more about the other teachers who joined her in the teachers' room.

There was Nura, who taught biology to the tenth and eleventh grades in the scientific section. Nura was always friendly and helpful, even though the other teachers told her to rest because she was pregnant with her fifth child. She was hoping it would be a girl; she always said that girls are so much nicer and easier to deal with than boys.

Whenever Nura talked about how much she preferred to have a girl, Fatin would get upset. Fatin had three girls and she prayed with all her heart that her next baby would be a boy. Every time she met a woman who had borne sons, she would start an interrogation with her in order to find out what this woman did differently and how she managed to get pregnant with a boy.

Abrar always opposed Fatin. Abrar taught religion and she would constantly criticise Fatin and remind her that the gender of an unborn child could only be determined by Allah. Only Allah knew what was good for a believer, and Allah would give people what was good for them. Abrar had eight sons and deep in her heart she wished for a daughter. Her husband had a good relationship with his sons; though he was strict, he tried to be fair to all of them. So as not to compromise the morals of his sons, Abrar's husband allowed only one TV in the house, and it was in his and Abrar's bedroom.

Abrar told the teachers, "Look how bad the world has become. All the crime and bad behaviour come from watching satellite television. We have to protect our children. Our kids watch TV, they see bad behaviour, and then they try to imitate it. Look at what's happening on the streets when young men pursue girls. This behaviour doesn't come from our Islamic culture, that's the influence of the West. Teach your kids good Islamic behaviour."

Since her sons had got older, Abrar noticed that she had less of an influence on them. Her house was a man's world, in which there was little place for her.

Albandary taught Arabic. Because she spent at least two periods a day in the same classroom, she was the one who really knew every student. When she talked with the students about literature, she always managed to find a way to drift from the subject and talk about personal matters. But she never talked to the other teachers about the students' personal lives. Albandary believed, like Abrar, that it was a sin to gossip about people. The line between gossip and trying to understand a person was very thin, so it was better not to say anything at all. Albandary came from one of the big clans, a clan to which many of the students belonged, too. Only when she felt that one of her students was really being treated unfairly would she interfere with another teacher. Often she would take a girl aside and talk to her in private if she felt that she had a problem.

Huda was not married, so the teachers would not talk in front of her about sexuality or problems they might be having with their husbands. Huda was maybe forty-years-old, considered an old spinster in Arabic culture. She never told anybody her age, and if someone asked how many years of experience she had teaching, she would laugh and say that she had just started last year. And everybody knew that it was not true.

Muneera taught geography, but she was not highly motivated for her work as a teacher. What she loved was to sit at the table in the middle of the room, drink coffee, gossip, and tell jokes. She had a real talent in turning every event into a joke. Recently, she had complained about her husband. According to her, he spent more time with the computer than with her. He would even spend the night with the computer instead of spending it with her.

Muneera suspected that he had put his savings in the stock market. More and more he would ask her for money or tell her to pay a bill. Muneera didn't want to spend her salary on paying bills. The other teachers got her stirred up over this. They told her not to even consider spending her money on the household; the expenses of the household were the duty of the husband, they said. If she would pay the bills, he would save his money, and soon he'd have enough to get a second wife. Albandary advised Muneera to increase her expenses. Money problems were the best way to prevent a husband from getting another wife.

And then there was Rajah. Rajah taught home economics and because of that, all the students loved her. There was no easier subject – failing wasn't even a possibility. Rajah loved her students; she was prepared to defend them at any moment. In her students, Rajah saw her own teenage daughter; she considered it her duty as a mother and a teacher to spoil them.

When Rajah was eighteen-years-old and had just finished school, a suitor came to her family. She was happy and excited that finally she could start living her own life. Immediately she gave her consent to the marriage. Later she would say that she never learnt to love her husband, and at eighteen-years-old, she also didn't have the patience to wait for love to grow. Soon after the birth of her daughter, she asked for a divorce. She returned to her parent's house with her daughter, but she knew that her ex-husband would take her daughter away from her in case she got married again.

For this reason, she always said she'd only get married after she had married off her daughter.

After her mother died of cancer, Rajah lived with her father and brother.

Because her parents had always urged her to, Rajah had invested her money, and together the family members had bought a house. Her brother and his wife and children lived on the ground floor while Rajah, her father, and her daughter lived on the first floor. But a year after his wife died of cancer, Rajah's father had a heart attack and died on the same day. Thereafter Rajah felt a great emptiness. She would often sit and look at the chair her father used to sit in.

She remembered his laugh and the protection she had felt from him when he was alive. Her brother was three years younger than she, and he didn't have the wisdom her father had shown.

After her father's death, Rajah's life continued with much the same routine. Life now revolved around her daughter and school. But to an increasing extent, she felt a strange longing, a longing for life, for happiness, for pain, for worries, for laughter – for passion. Was this all life had to offer her? A daughter and a job? Was it her destiny to wait for her daughter to be old enough to marry, and then her life was over? That was all there was?

To escape the routine and take advantage of her free time, Rajah enrolled in a computer course for women only. After that she bought a computer and spent the long evening hours in online chat rooms. It was there that she Essam.

From the beginning Essam told her that he was married and had three kids, the fourth one on its way. His wife, Assma, was his cousin. For their families it had always been a fact that one day Essam would marry Assma. In the beginning of their married life together, everything was normal, no ups and no downs, a straight line – no surprises, because they had known each other since childhood. And Essam was a nice guy; what the family wanted of him, Essam did; what Assma wanted, Essam did.

But as the years went by, Essam felt that he was in a cage; there was never room for Essam the person. His relationship with Assma never changed. They liked each other, they respected each other, but there was no passion in their relationship. Assma got accustomed to getting her own way; her interest in the children and her husband was limited. The maid did the cooking, the washing, the cleaning, and she looked after the children. When Assma got up, at noon, she dressed, put on her make-up, and left the house to visit her mother or her sisters. Every day, the sisters would meet in a different house. Sometimes they would go shopping together or they would sit and talk or visit friends. In the afternoon, Assma would return home to take a nap and take a turn looking after the children because at night she would leave the house once again to visit other friends.

Soon after Essam met Rajah, he complained to her about his life and the dissatisfaction he had felt. He was happy when he could talk to Rajah. Later, they wouldn't really remember who first brought up the idea of a misyar marriage, a marriage which only a limited number of people would know about, and in which couples live separately but get together periodically, often for sexual relations. Essam didn't want to have an actual second wife because he was afraid of Assma and her mother, and he wanted to avoid problems with them. His mother-in-law was also his aunt, his father's sister, and in the case of a second wife she would do everything in her power to make Essam's life a living hell.

Rajah wanted a husband, somebody with whom she could be intimate and who would give her the kind of tenderness nobody else was able to give her. Even if he wouldn't be there every day, her waiting hours would be filled with a new purpose and with expectations. Having a husband would fill the emptiness inside her.

After Rajah discussed Essam's proposal with her brother, the two men came together and they drew up the marriage contract. Rajah would not ask for anything from Essam. Essam would visit her every few days, whenever he had time to spare, but he would not be obliged to support her in any way. They agreed on not having any children. That was Rajah's condition. She also wanted to keep the marriage a secret because she was afraid that her daughter's father would learn about the new marriage and he would then take her daughter away from her. And they agreed that in case their secret marriage didn't work out, they would break up and go their separate ways.

Nobody in school knew anything about Rajah and Essam getting married, or when he visited her for the first time. Rajah's friends and colleagues only noticed that Rajah seemed changed. She was always well dressed and her make-up was applied with a lot of care. Some days they would hear her laugh even before they saw her enter a room, and when she was in the room, the mood would be different: happy, funny. Everybody would start joking around.

The teachers started to whisper: "What has changed Rajah? Why is she so happy?"

Everybody tried to get to the bottom of Rajah's change. Latifa thought that it might have to do with a man, but Abrar rejected that idea because she said that Rajah was a pious woman, she would never get involved with a man. So the teachers tried to get the secret out of Fatin, who was Rajah's closest friend since they had gone to university together. But Fatin told them that she had no clue.

In time, the teachers grew accustomed to seeing Rajah happy and laughing and joking with everybody on certain days. On these days she would often bring her homemade specialties, which everybody had to taste. And then there were the other days, when Rajah was sad and tired and hardly looked up from her desk. On those days, her mobile would rarely ring until suddenly everything changed, and once again Rajah was happy, laughing, and joking.

9.

"*Salam*, Susie! Today, you and I have *monawba*", Nura told her one morning as Susie was about to enter the teachers' room.
"Monawba? What's that?"
"After school we sit behind the school gate to make sure that the girls are properly covered when they leave the school."
"And how long do we have to stay?"
"We stay as long as there are students in school. It can last for up to two hours, if we're lucky."

After the last period, Susie met Nura at the school gate. Nura had brought two students' chairs. As the bell rang, the gate was opened from the outside. The girls stormed out of the school premises; they had put on their abayas and covered their faces. They each knew somebody would be waiting for them. The gateway was crowded with girls trying to exit. The noise was earsplitting. Susie felt she couldn't breathe; it was hot, the air was full of dust, and all she could see were black figures. Through a microphone came the voice of a man.
"Ahmed, Ahmed Alzaharani", called the voice.
"Why does he call the name of a boy? We don't have boys in the school?" Susie asked.
"Some people think that it's improper to say a woman's name in public. For those people, women and everything that has anything to do with women has a sexual aura. So they call the name of a brother or the father."

From time to time, Nura would stop a student.

"Cover your face properly; I can see you through your veil."
"Put your abaya on your head. If you put your abaya on your shoulders, the men outside will recognize your figure."
"Your veil has too many ornaments. It draws the attention of men. Tomorrow bring another one."
A girl entered the school. Nura stopped her.
"Where do you come from?"
"I've just left the school, I thought my father was waiting outside but he hasn't come yet."
"You know it's not allowed for students to leave the school and then come back. Who knows where you've been. Maybe you didn't attend school today."
"No, truly, *Abla*, I was in school all day. Ask my teachers."
"Okay, this time I'll believe you, but don't do it again."

Some students walked around in the schoolyard. Many walked in pairs, sometimes arm-in-arm. They all seemed absorbed in conversation.

A few girls sat in groups on carpets that somebody had brought to school some time ago. They laughed and joked around, apparently having a good time. In front of them were bags of potato chips and other junk food; most girls had a soft drink, too.

One group especially grabbed Nura's attention. She told Susie to watch them. They had put their heads together and seemed to be oblivious to their surroundings. From time to time, they looked up. Then they looked at Susie spitefully and continued talking. Susie knew one of the girls, Hanan, the girl who sat in the last row of her class.

"I wish I were once again that young", Nura said. "Being a student, going to school – what a great time. No worries, no responsibilities."

"Really?" Susie said. "I thought it was a difficult time. We had to decide what we wanted to do with the rest of our lives, what kind of profession we wanted. Many of my classmates had boyfriends. That, too, brought certain responsibilities; should they consider marrying him? Was he good? Did he treat her well? I think it was the most difficult time of my life. Any decision I made would influence the rest of my life."

Nura looked at her unbelievingly. "But what about your parents? Didn't they tell you what to do?"

"They gave me suggestions, but I had to make the decisions. I had the responsibility for making my own choices, which meant I could never blame anybody but myself."

"No, for us it was different", replied Nura. "In this age, a girl has almost no responsibilities. My father decided which man I should marry. He told me to marry the man who came to him to ask for my hand in marriage. I know I can trust my father completely, he knows what's good for me better than I do. And for my profession – that, too, is mostly not for us to decide. It depends largely on marks in school. If you have excellent grades, you can go to university to study medicine or computers. Many girls don't want to study medicine because then they have to work in a mixed environment, and many people think that's immoral. So they prefer to become a teacher and work in an all-female environment. I think being a teacher and a mother is closer to what Allah intended for us."

There were still twenty students left in the schoolyard.

Nura got up. She walked over to a group of girls and told them to go home.

"Please, *Abla* let me stay a little longer with my friends. I only see them in school and we are not allowed to talk in class."

"Why? You can phone them."

"My father is very strict. He doesn't allow me to use the phone. We also don't have Internet. My father believes it's not suitable for a girl to use the phone or the Internet. The devil could whisper in her ear to use it to chat with men."

"And you? What do you think?"

"I don't know. Everybody is talking about it. But if my father says it's bad for me, he's probably right. He only wants what is good for me."

Finally, there were only two girls left.

"Why are you still here?" Nura asked one of them. "At what time are you being picked up?"

"I wait for my brothers, they should have been here long ago", answered the girl. Susie knew her; it was Arwa, one of her students in the scientific section, a polite, friendly girl.

"Susie, can you please go with the girls?" asked Nura. "Let them call their fathers so they can remind them to pick them up. But be careful. Make sure they really phone the house and not another number."

Shortly after that, the last students were picked up. Quiet descended on the school. The yard in front of them was covered with trash the girls had left behind, the sun glinting on some discarded soda cans. A soft breeze played with a page in a book; papers taken out of notebooks were lying around. But everything was calm, even peaceful. Another day in the lives of the women who attended this school had passed.

Tomorrow, it would once again be loud, busy, crowded.

"Come, Susie, we can go home," Nura said. "Outside, the men of the cleaning crew are waiting. And my driver is there. Tell me where you live, and I'll drop you off. This way you don't have to wait for your husband, and I'll know where you live."

The next morning, while she was on the way to her classroom, Susie met up with the school's director. *Abla* Hessa looked at her, and after exchanging greetings she asked Susie to follow her to her office. There, she closed the door, sat down in one of the chairs in front of her desk, and asked Susie to take a seat in the other chair. After asking her some polite questions about her well-being, *Abla* Hessa told Susie that she had received phone calls from some fathers. They had complained that the English lessons included some singing, and if this should happen again they would go to the Ministry of Education and complain. As if it wasn't enough that a Westerner taught their daughters, one of them had said.

"But we didn't sing", Susie responded. "I only taught the girls jazz chants. That's a method to learn the intonation of the English language. Most of the girls enjoyed it", Susie told *Abla* Hessa in her broken Arabic.

"I know that you mean well, but we consider singing and making music a sin, and I cannot tolerate it in school."

"Through the chanting, the students were having a lot of fun", Susie continued. "You should have seen them – everybody was participating, even the students in the last row. Why does learning and school have to always be so strict? Let them have some fun once in a while."

"You heard what I said" *Abla* Hessa replied. "My hands are tied. If somebody complains against you officially, I cannot help you. I don't tolerate singing in my school, and that's it."

Susie realised that there was nothing she could do and she left the room. No wonder the students were not motivated. In each and every period, the teacher was supposed to explain, next to grammatical items or reading, at least twenty new words that the girls should then know by heart. That was too much. Most students gave up before they had even started to learn. But Susie believed that learning in itself was motivation. She still remembered the first time she actually felt it herself. As a student in school, Susie had never liked English or the other subjects for that matter. Even today, she could remember the frustration she had experienced when she didn't understand the teacher and had felt that the beautiful aspects of life were passing her by. Success? A word she hardly knew. Pleasure in learning? Why?

One day, during an English lesson, her teacher talked about Robert Frost and one of his poems. Barely did Susie understand the meaning of the poem, which was about a route that went through a forest. Susie loved nature, trees, and flowers, and now she realised that there was an American poet who had talked about all of this. For homework, the teacher told them to write their impressions of the poem. But this time, Susie didn't want to give up; she wanted to do the homework, no matter how difficult. The teacher advised her to use a dictionary. Susie spent all afternoon and part of the night translating the poem in order to understand it. After that, everything fell into place. Later, Susie never forgot this first moment of success, a success she had achieved all on her own. There and then she began to believe that there was nothing she couldn't do; she only had to put her mind to it.

But how could she convey this feeling, this experience, to her Arab students?

Susie decided to go her own way in dealing with the students, it seemed impossible to persuade the others that her ideas of learning and teaching in this environment were correct. But even if she could only make a change for one student, wouldn't it be worth it? It was evident that the system was successful for some students, but what about the others? Didn't everyone deserve a chance?

Susie decided on the middle path – to encourage students to feel that learning can be enjoyable, but at the same time she would expect more self-discipline from her students. In an environment where learning was associated with strictness, memorisation, and obedience, she couldn't expect students or the school's administration to understand her point of view. But she could make her lessons more personal, and she could try to get her students to talk about themselves and their problems without feeling as though it was inappropriate. And why shouldn't she tell the girls about life in the Western world, including its shortcomings? They knew all about the freedoms there, but they didn't know about the responsibilities.

Susie began by trying to memorise the names of her students, so that instead of 'you' she would say 'Hessa', 'Muneera', or 'Mona'. And instead of explaining grammatical items in an impersonal setting, she would use the names of the students to form a sentence out of their environment.

"Hessa eats *kabsa*, Hessa has eaten *kabsa*, Hessa ate *kabsa*, Hessa wants to eat *kabsa*."

"But, teacher, I don't like kabsa. I want hamburger", protested Hessa.

At the end of each lesson, Susie tried to keep some time left for discussion. In the beginning, Susie insisted that the students discuss everything in English.

"Think in English, then you can speak it. Even if you make mistakes, who cares?"

Sometimes, when a girl who was weak in English tried to speak, her friends would help her, but sometimes when the subject they talked about was very emotional, they all started talking, usually in Arabic.

Most of the questions the students asked her were about how she'd met her husband. Was it romantic? Was life in the Western world just like the way they showed in American movies – everything easy and happy ever after?

Often the students would talk about religion. They believed that Islam gave them rights they weren't being allowed to use. They knew that Saudi society was not ready yet to give them the rights the Prophet had talked about 1400 years ago. Often people would look at traditions and consider them to be part of Islam, forgetting that they were simply *interpretations* of the religion that had been passed down. Most men and women would not distinguish between the two, and therefore didn't know what was subject to change in the practise of Islam.

10.

Dear Gitta,

Thank you for your letter. The life you're telling me about is so far removed, it's like life on another planet — I feel as if I were on the moon!

Since I arrived here, I have been thinking about becoming a Muslim, I mean a real Muslim, not only on paper. You know that in order to marry Ahmed, he asked me to convert to Islam at least on paper because it made my coming to Saudi Arabia easier. But even before I met Ahmed, I wasn't a good Christian; there were too many questions that were unanswered for me. I never understood the concept of the Trinity in Christianity: Father, Son and the Holy Ghost. Also, I always believed that Jesus is the son of God, but I think of him as a person, a great Prophet, but is he God? Like many people I know, I thought it's easier to stay away from religion; for me the concept was too complicated to really understand it, it wasn't logical. I never found satisfactory answers to all my questions, everybody always told me "Don't ask." So, I put religion aside, as a subject I didn't like to think about.

I met Ahmed, and I asked him questions; he always tried to find an answer for me. Even when we were still living in Germany, my ideas about religion changed, but I never thought about taking the final step and commiting to the faith.

My ideas started to change when I arrived in Riyadh. Here, religion is part of the day-to-day life, one cannot ignore it. Wherever you are, you always hear the five calls for prayer. Also, what made me change was my mother-in-law. I often watch her when she deals with Samia, her oldest daughter. Samia has good days and bad days. On her bad days, it's difficult to be around her. Sometimes she verbally attacks her mother. I don't understand her, but once I asked my mother-in-law why she was so upset. Fatima told me that on her bad days, Samia quarrels with her fate and her handicap. Often she blames her mother. But her mother always keeps quiet, she tells her that what happened was Allah's will, and His ways cannot be understood by us. We only have to trust.

I think you understand how tedious life can be in a big family. But Fatima never loses her calm or strength. My mother-in-law stays composed in the most difficult situations. Often she won't participate in discussions, but retreats to her room to pray. She told me once that she gets inner tranquillity from praying and submitting herself to Allah and His will.

I like this attitude – it made me think about life and what I want to achieve. I realised that I need a belief system that gives me strength.

I also want to have a feeling of belonging. Who am I, why am I here, where am I going?

I have moments where I get really upset; I feel it's all too much: living in a strange country, in a big family without the familiarity of my previous life. I have moments when I get frustrated, I want to take something and break it, I feel like ants are crawling all over my body and don't know what to do. I want to explode!

But - I have to restrain myself. Imagine how it would look if I exploded! Recently, I noticed that when I get angry, I talk to myself in German. Often I do it without being aware of it. Yesterday, Fatima and Samia looked at me because they didn't know why I was upset. I was ashamed.

One day, I forget what had unsettled me, I saw Fatima praying, and I felt this urge to do the same. I asked her how I should pray and she showed me. Since then, whenever it's prayer time, she calls me and I get "on-the-job-training."

It's true, right now I don't know much about Islam, its teachings and ideologies. But when I pray, I feel secure, happy, and at peace with myself. I get a sense of purification.

What is it that brought me here? Is there really something that's called fate? Will I be able to forget my previous life and become a good Muslim and a good Saudi?

I feel so much better now since I started practicing Islam. Praying calms me, it gives me solace and comfort. Why do I worry? My life is in the hands of Allah. Allah knows what is good for me.

When I stand among praying women, I feel I belong!
I miss you.
Take care,
Susie

11.

A rustle, a medley of noises, then came the voice of *Abla* Hessa over the intercom:

"I wish you the best for the whole year. If tomorrow is Ramadan, then school will start at 9:30 a.m. All teachers and students must be in school at that time. The first period will start at 9:45; school will be over at 2:30 p.m., *in sha Allah*."

Everybody in Susie's classroom started talking at the same time.

"Do you think tomorrow is Ramadan?"

"I hope so, I love Ramadan!"

"What do you like about Ramadan?" Susie asked her students.

"Ramadan is a beautiful month", Kholoud explained to her. "We feel closer to Allah. Every day, our self-control is tested: Will I succeed in fasting? Won't I give in to the feeling of hunger or thirst? We feel connected to Muslims everywhere who are all fasting at this moment with us. We are all hungry, thirsty, and tired."

Wafa said, "Fasting is the only service we really do for Allah. Nobody can detect for sure if we're fasting or not. When we pray, or when we cover ourselves up with the abaya and the veil, people see us and they say 'Look how pious she is, she's praying all day long'. But we could eat secretly and nobody would find out. Only Allah would know."

"I like the feast at the end of Ramadan", another girl said. "After we haven't eaten from sunrise to sunset for a whole month, there is a big feast. We'll get new clothes and gifts."

Someone else piped up, "During Ramadan, everything is different, as if we're on vacation. Our daily habits are changed. All day long I wait for sunset, everything else is unimportant. I only wait for this moment when I can eat the first date and take the first sip of milk."

That night, they announced on TV that the new moon was seen. Ramadan had started.

People congratulated one another: "All the best for the year. May Allah accept our fasting."

Soon afterwards, they heard the call to the night prayer over the loudspeakers of the mosques.

After most people had slept for a short time, they got up at 4 a.m. to eat. Parents reminded their children not to eat anything that would make them thirsty. Then they had a last sip of water. The call for the morning prayer came over the loudspeakers of the mosques and was loud enough to be heard by all. Following prayer, people went to bed, only to get up at 9 a.m., ready for work.

The first day of Ramadan was usually the most difficult: no breakfast, no coffee, no tea, no cigarettes – until the sun had set, and then the first sip of coffee was delicious, like nothing else tasted ever before.

When Susie came home from school, Fatima and Samia were in the kitchen preparing the *futur*, the meal they would eat as soon as they heard the call for the sunset prayer. Fatima had cooked soup and boiled the *fava* beans. She had also prepared the dough and the meat filling for the sambosaks. Samia had decided to cook *mahshi*, zucchinis filled with rice and meat. Susie wanted to help her, but Samia refused. Fatima noticed that Susie was antsy, so she suggested that she prepare the dessert: strawberry Jell-O with vanilla sauce. After Susie had finished, she sat down at the kitchen table next to

Fatima, who showed her how to form the sambosaks before they baked them in the oven.

When they heard the call for prayer, everything was ready.

They ended their fast with dates and milk; the family prayed together and then started eating. They were all hungry. Susie didn't know what to eat first, everything looked so delicious.

Ahmed laughed: "Your eyes are bigger than your stomach. Slow down, you've got all night to eat."

Once they had eaten, they all took a nap before Fatima, Samia, and Ahmed went to the mosque for night prayer.

When they returned, Susie had some tea prepared for all of them. And then Suad, Salwa, and Zainab arrived with their families. Suad brought a big tray of *konafa*, a special sweet with nuts, very thin dough, and lots of sugar, which they all finished very quickly. Salwa insisted they should all come to her house the next day, but Zainab got upset. She wanted to be the first one to invite the family. Finally, they agreed that they would first visit Salwa and then eat at Zainab's house the day after.

Fatima cooked rice *bukhari*, a dish with rice, nuts and raisins, for the morning meal before they started fasting again.

All the women helped clean the kitchen. They had just washed the last plate when they heard the first call to prayer. It was time to get a last sip of water.

The next few days were easier than Susie had thought they would be. In fact, a day would pass so quickly that she could hardly feel thirst or hunger. By the second week, Susie sensed fasting was more difficult, but it wasn't as much the hunger and the thirst as it was the fatigue; she only wanted to sleep a night through without having to get up to eat and then go back to sleep with a full stomach.

But she noticed that her colleagues at the school had no problems with this routine.

"Because we're accustomed to fasting; it gets easier", Latifa told her.

On the second Tuesday, one day before the weekend, Susie felt exhausted, thirsty, and hungry. She was tired of everything and only wanted the weekend to come as quickly as possible.

"We learnt as children to fast", Nura told her. "When I was five- or six-years-old, I wanted to fast. My mother didn't want to discourage me, so she told me I could fast. Then, once a day, usually around noon, my mother gave me something to eat. After that I continued fasting. The first time I fasted the whole day, my parents gave me a gift. You can't imagine how proud I was. Fasting is easier for us, we're accustomed to it. Lie down and take a rest, then it will be easier for you, too."

This day, at sunset, Susie felt that she had accomplished her goal of not giving in to her cravings; she had the feeling that she had grown stronger, that even she could overcome hunger and thirst like her colleagues.

The last days of Ramadan were filled with the preparations for the big feast. First, Fatima insisted that they clean the house and get rid of all the old, useless stuff. Then they acquired new clothes, and finally, sweets, chocolate, nuts, and cake were bought for the feast, the celebration to mark the end of Ramadan.

This year, Fatima wanted to celebrate in a big way. At last, all her children, their spouses, and her grandchildren were reunited. Suad insisted that they should celebrate in her house. Only her house was big enough to hold them all, she said. On the first day of the feast she would prepare for a big party.

On the thirtieth day of Ramadan, they announced on TV that the new moon had been seen, and the holy month was coming to an end. After the announcement, they broadcasted music and showed smiling children wearing their new clothes. People everywhere congratulated one another.

"When are we going to see Suad?" Susie asked.
"After we get up and have breakfast."
"And at what time is that?"

"Who knows? Maybe at noon or at one o'clock. Why? Is it important?"

"Yes. We have to plan it."

"Some things can't be planned. You'll see."

Finally they were all ready to leave the house. Fatima and Samia wore new *galabias*, the traditional wide, embroidered dresses for women and new abayas over it. Fatima had insisted that Susie, too, buy herself a new dress. And in the morning, she surprised Susie with a new abaya, which was embroidered with colourful flowers. Susie had admired it in a store once, but it was too expensive for her and sadly she had to leave the store without buying it.

When they arrived, Suad had been burning expensive incense, so that even the house smelled like a feast. By and by, the other family members arrived, all in new dresses and with the scent of their new perfumes. They smelled so good that kissing one another in greeting was a real sensory pleasure.

On the table, Suad had placed different kinds of dates, expensive chocolate, cakes filled with dates and nuts, sweets, roasted nuts, and sunflower kernels. After they all sat down, they were welcomed with fresh-pressed juice and Arabic coffee, followed by tea. In-between they tried out the different kinds of sweets from the table.

Susie couldn't make up her mind what to taste first, but then she decided to take a piece from each plate. She especially liked the *labania*, a white specialty from Mecca that looked and tasted like marzipan but much sweeter.

Following the night prayer, when it was cooler outside, Suad asked them to come to the rooftop, she had a surprise for everyone.

The flat roof of the house had been decorated with garlands and lanterns. In the center of the roof was a long table with chairs placed around it. Suad's laptop with a projector was on a small table in the right-hand corner, and across from that she had put up a white screen.

They sat down on the chairs, and Suad made sure that all of

Fatima's grandchildren were present. Then she started with the display of pictures. She had put all the old family photos she could find on the computer. There were photos of Fatima and her children; Ahmed as a small boy with short pants; Samia as a serious teenager between some other family members; Suad, very skinny, looking skeptically into the lens; Salwa with her hair plaited; and Zainab on her new bicycle when she was six-years-old. Susie was surprised how little they had all changed. They were older and a little bit heavier, but she could still recognize each of them easily from their childhood photos.

Then came the pictures of the grandchildren. Photos of each one of them were shown, with nobody left out. Suad asked the family to tell something they remembered about each grandchild. After that, the show was interrupted when each grandchild was asked to come before the whole family, where they were given a gift. The children were excited, they all wanted to go first. *What were they going to say about them?* Amal, Suad's younger daughter, hoped it wouldn't be something embarrassing. *And what was the gift?*

Fatima was the center of the show; again and again there came a picture showing her, and every time they kissed and hugged her, showing her how much she meant to all of them. With each hug, Fatima told them what a beautiful feast it was for her, being with her children and grandchildren was a feast in itself.

After all the gifts had been distributed, it was time to eat. Suad had arranged a buffet at the other corner of the roof. There was rice with cooked lamb, salad, and grilled fish. On another table they found crème caramel and two black forest cakes, naturally without liquor.

Suad's daughters helped their mother serve their guests. Amal went around with a tray with rice and meat; Haifa was responsible for juice, soft drinks, and water. Every time the girls tried to sit down to eat, they were hit by a glance from Suad, so immediately they got up again to serve the guests. Their cousins didn't feel like eating without them so they, too, got up to help Amal and Haifa.

Because the boys were all around the same age, they sat together and tried to annoy the girls. Every time they saw one of the girls sitting down they called out for water, meat, or dessert. Susie could see how annoyed the girls were becoming. Haifa went to Suad to complain about the boys, but Suad ignored her.

"You're a girl", she told her. "You have to learn to make your guests feel welcome in the house. They are boys. One day they'll be responsible for you, so respect them."

Following supper, they drank green tea, and then it was time to go home.

"Tomorrow, you'll come to our place, don't forget", Salwa and Ali called out as they were leaving the house.

12.

"Susie, would you like to get together with us after school? A new café shop for women only has just opened in the mall", Mona asked her in English. "Latifa is coming and so is Nura. Latifa teaches English, you know her, and Nura has lived with her husband in the States, so you can speak to her in English, too."

In the afternoon, Ahmed drove her to the mall where they were going to meet. As they were driving, Susie noticed for the first time the palm trees and bushes that grew in the middle of the streets. Why hadn't she noticed them before? The green trees were still nothing to compare to German trees, but she wasn't in Europe; she now lived in the middle of the desert, where water was scarce.

They stopped at a red traffic light and Susie looked at the palm tree next to her. How many sandstorms had the tree survived? The tree's roots were anchored deeply in the soil. Susie wished she had roots like that, anchored here in this soil. But she still felt out of place – a stranger, an imported tree with no roots. Would she ever succeed in having roots anchored here?

She explained to Ahmed that Mona and her driver would bring her home, so there was no need for him to pick her up from the mall because she didn't know how long they would be meeting.

Susie arrived first. She walked around the mall. Even here in

Saudi Arabia, the summer had come to an end. In Europe and the United States, fall had started. Most of the shops in the mall were filled with winter clothing. Susie wondered who would buy the fur jackets and the sweaters. She still felt the heat; at noon the outside temperature even now was thirty-five degrees centigrade. Only inside the mall was it cool because of the central air conditioning.

Susie heard her name being called and turned around. From the voice she recognised Mona standing behind her, a figure totally covered in black. Together they went to the third floor, which was reserved for women only. At the stairs and the elevator leading up, security guards were standing, making sure that no men would, intentionally or inadvertently, go upstairs.

On the third floor, Mona removed her veil and uncovered her hair. As always, she looked stunning with her black hair, brown eyes, and impeccable figure. She wore black pants and a simple blouse, but one could see that the simple outfit was expensive.

All the women on the floor had uncovered their faces. Some kept their hair covered, and most of them still wore their abayas. Susie and Mona chose a table in one of the small coffee shops and gave their order to a Filipino waitress just before Latifa arrived. Nura was half an hour late; her children hadn't wanted her to leave, and then, when she was finally ready to leave, the driver couldn't be found. He had gone to the banque to send money to his family in Sri Lanka without telling her and had been delayed, she said.

Susie watched the other women in the mall. Some had brought their children, their small sons and older daughters. Some teenagers were walking around with their friends. Most of the girls were dressed in western clothes – tight jeans and t-shirts with inscriptions from Disneyland, San Diego Zoo, or Paris. A few t-shirts displayed English expressions; Susie wondered if they knew what they implied.

She felt Mona's glance and looked back at her. She hadn't noticed that Nura was talking to them. She told them about her oldest son who was having problems in school. He didn't want to accept the authority of the teacher, who insisted on being respected. Nura said that he wasn't competent in raising young boys.

"Why aren't you married", Susie asked Mona.

Mona told them that she was supposed to marry her cousin; for years the family had been insisting on the marriage. But she had always found reasons to delay it. He was the son of her uncle, the brother of her father. They had known each other since they played together as young children, but Mona had never liked him. She thought he was superficial and uneducated. He was only interested in his business and his friends, whom he met regularly on the weekends. He was three years older than she was. Her cousin had left school after completing junior high and had worked with his father ever since. In the last few years they had changed their business, to importing goods from China, which they sold in two-riyal stores where customers could buy everything on a low budget. Business had developed very well, and Mona's uncle had made a lot of money. But Mona wanted more than money; she wanted a soul mate, a husband who could read her mind.

She had found her soul mate in Osama, the brother of her best friend. She had met him one day when she was visiting her friend. Osama had thought that his sister was alone and entered her room without knocking. After that initial encounter, he would sometimes answer the phone when Mona called to talk to her friend, and so it had happened that they bonded. Osama had studied in the States, and Mona felt that he was all that she had been looking for in her future husband. He had only one minus: he didn't belong to a tribe, and there was this unwritten rule in Mona's tribe that their women could only marry true tribesmen.

Mona had saved Osama's number in her mobile under a girl's name so that in case her father or her mother would at any time pick up her mobile, they wouldn't get suspicious. Only Osama's sister knew about their love.

As Mona was talking about her love of Osama, Susie could sense how much he meant to her.

"I know that he's the love of my life. I belong to those people who only love once in their life, and this love means everything to me. Either I marry this man or I don't want to get married."

Nura consoled her. She told them that in the beginning she

didn't like her husband, either. Her marriage had been arranged by her aunt, her husband was a distant relative of her. Her father had approved of him. In his opinion, the two of them matched well, and he had talked Nura into marrying him. But they only became close during their honeymoon when Nura noticed that he was different than her first impression of him.

"Today, I can't imagine my life without him", Nura said. "Sometimes, when he's on a business trip, our longing for each other becomes so strong that we talk for a long time on the phone. We count the hours till we are together again. Who would have thought that at the beginning of our married life?"

"That's because you have children, so your life together has a purpose", Latifa said. They looked at one another in dismay; in all their talking they hadn't considered Latifa's feelings and the fact that Latifa didn't have children. She had tried everything; she'd visited three different fertility clinics, but after all the examinations and several small operations, she'd been told that the chance for a pregnancy could never be 100 percent.

"Susie, why don't you have children?"

"I don't know. We went to a doctor and he said that everything is okay, no problems, but ... I don't know."

"You need patience. Sometimes it takes time."

Susie laughed: "I have patience, and I think my husband has, too. But the problem is his family. They always look at my belly and ask every month."

"I know what you mean", Latifa said. "Let's change the subject. I want to have fun. Let's talk about something amusing. Does anybody know a new joke?"

"I know one", Mona said.

"A cross-eyed Bedouin wanted to marry a second wife; then accidentally he married his first one again."

Latifa and Susie looked at each other.

"Don't you know a better one?"

"A man in Cairo asked his daughter, who had just taken her driver's licence test, if she had passed. The daughter answered: 'I don't know; the examiner is in the hospital.'"

"That sounds like a Saudi joke; women are too stupid to drive."

"Okay, what about this one. A man from upper Egypt was in Sharm el Sheikh for vacation, and he sent his family a picture of himself in bathing trunks on the beach. His family immediately sent him some clothes."

"Those are stupid jokes. Susie, tell us about your life before coming here and your family. Why did you marry a Saudi?"

"That's not an easy question to answer. It has to do with my upbringing, I think."

"Tell us. We want to hear everything."

Susie began: "My father was already divorced twice when he met my mother; they were both middle aged. My mother was a teacher. My father could be a very charming man if he wanted to. He was the only child of very rich parents and had had a very spoiled upbringing. But through two world wars they had lost all their wealth, and when the last money disappeared, so did his second wife. My mother had compassion for this man. He was like a big boy who needed her, and my mother wanted to be needed.

"They got married, but when my brother was born, my mother was overwhelmed by her love for her child; she hadn't imagined that she could love like that. Then my brother died suddenly from an accident. My mother's pain was so huge that she disregarded her surroundings completely. My father felt alone with his hurt. Around this time he met a woman, attractive, intelligent, unmarried, with a career and money of her own, who knew exactly what she wanted. Suddenly, there were three people in my parents' marriage.

"My father used to visit the other woman regularly; it was as if she was his second wife. Once, in the beginning, my mother went to this woman and told her, 'You can have him, he's all yours'. But the other woman laughed and said that she didn't want to have him as a husband, he would just run back to my mother anyway, she was too important to him.

"After some time, my mother noticed that her period had stopped. She thought it was because of menopause. But then her belly became bigger. When she realised that she was pregnant again, she was devastated, she didn't want another child. And she felt too old to raise a child. And what if this child would also die after she had started to love it? But she didn't know where to get an abortion, and she also thought it was a sin to abort.

"I was born, and as she held me in her arms for the first time, she swore that I was smiling at her.

"When I was eighteen-years-old, my mother got an attack and died in the same night. She had always told me about her life, that she didn't want me to make wrong choices like she had at times. We were very close and I loved her more than I can describe, she was everything to me. Suddenly she wasn't there any more, and instead there was a huge emptiness. A few months later, I met Ahmed, and so I transferred all this love I had in me to another person. Since the day we met, we have always been together. I think, as an Arab who grew up with older sisters, he felt responsible for me."

"What about your relatives, your uncles, aunts, cousins? Do you see them often?"

"No, I hardly know my relatives. Most of them were already older when I grew up, and they lived in another city. I don't really have anybody in Germany, maybe a childhood friend, Gitta, but she has her own busy life. The only real friend I have is much older than me. Christa has been married for many years to an American and she lives in the States."

"Is your father still alive?"

"He died last year. He'd been together with this other woman until his death. I know her well, she's nice. But I've always promised myself I'd never endure what my mother had to go through."

"Why not? A second wife also has its advantages", Latifa said. "I'm thinking about getting my husband a second wife. He wants to have children. I feel that he's unhappy."

"How can you do that?"

"A time will come when he'll want to get married. But when I choose a wife for him and they get married, then the two of them will feel indebted to me and they'll never get the idea to put me aside. And when I do it wisely, I can become a mother to his children, so I can still be a mother."

"Why don't you adopt?" Susie asked.

"In Islam it's not allowed to adopt children. We should, and we do, take care of children who are not our own, but we shouldn't adopt them. The name of a person can't be changed. Like my name is Latifa Abdullah, that's the name of my father, Ibrahim, that's my grandfather, Mohammed, my great grandfather, Abdulmajid, my great-great grandfather. So my complete name is Latifa Abdullah Ibrahim Mohammed Abdulmajid Alharby. This name is part of me, that's who I am", she said.

Then she explained that if she and her husband would take in a girl, one day there would be a gap between the girl and Latifa's husband because he wouldn't be her blood relative. "It's not allowed for a girl to live with a man who isn't her blood relative", Latifa said. The girl would be obliged to cover herself up all the time, because theoretically her father could marry her one day when she was old enough. And if they took in a boy child, because Latifa couldn't nurse him, it would not be appropriate for her to take him in her arms because she wouldn't be a blood relative of such a boy child.

"But that's so complicated", Susie said.

"Really? I think it's logical. We've been living like this for more than a thousand years, so these regulations come naturally. What we do very often is that we take care of orphaned children in our family or children whose parents got divorced and remarried another partner. One of my sisters grew up with my aunt. My mother took pity on her sister because she didn't have any children and my mother had six daughters. My sister loves my aunt; she always calls her Mama."

"Come, let's take a walk", Mona said.

"I have to go home", said Nura. "I have to check on my children's homework. Tomorrow, my oldest son has a test in hadith, the sayings of the Prophet. I don't believe that he memorised everything like he's supposed to."

"And I've to go, too. See you tomorrow in school", Latifa said. "My driver is at the entrance to the mall. I'll drop you off at your home, Susie."

13.

There was an unpleasant feeling in the air at school. It was even more difficult than usual to control the students. Nobody seemed to be eager to learn anything. Susie was exhausted. She sat down at her desk in the teachers' room and started correcting homework. Inside Hanan's notebook she found a drawing of a big red heart with *H*'s and *A*'s written inside. Susie made a huge question mark on the page and looked around for the homework, but except the *H*'s and *A*'s, there was nothing else in the notebook. She decided to talk to Hanan.

After a while Susie stopped. It seemed that the correcting never ended, always the same mistakes – fifty notebooks with the same mistakes in each one. Was there a main copy from where all the other copies came?

The teachers sat around the breakfast table, talking about the newest American injustice in the Middle East.

Suddenly Fatin said, "Before, I'd always seen the countries of the Western world as wanting to suppress us; they colonialised Africa and parts of Asia, and now they want to get their hands on our oil. I've seen movies but those were not real. Since Susie has come to us, Europe, and especially Germany, has got a face. I've never had contact with a Westerner before."

Huda agreed. "Yes, that's true."

"I wonder if there are in the West as many regional differences as we have here?" Fatin asked. "We all come from different parts of Saudi Arabia; we all have our different traditions that we brought with us from our hometowns to Riyadh. How is that in the West, Susie?"

At that moment, the newly installed fire siren started up. Another drill to check the alarm bell? But this time, the siren didn't stop. After two minutes, the teachers decided that there was something wrong.

"Do you remember? Last year there was a girls' school in Mecca that burned down. Some students died in the fire because the fire engines didn't arrive on time."

The voices in the corridor increased; the students, too, were in doubt. Susie decided to go downstairs to ask what was wrong with the siren.

Abla Hessa was standing with the other administration employees in front of her office, looking at the main switch of the siren, discussing why the siren could have started. Finally, the director decided to send three employees to check the classrooms for fire.

The whining of the siren still didn't stop.

Nobody could detect a fire. But the shrieking siren had lured the teachers and the students downstairs; they felt more secure standing next to the entrance of the school. Meanwhile, *Abla* Hessa decided to call the main administration office in downtown.

Albandary said it would be safer to open the secondary-school entrances.

But where were the keys? Abrar remembered that some time ago Muneera had participated in a fire drill and at that time she had to check all the keys.

"Muneera? Where's Muneera? She can help us!"

In the meantime, Abrar had found Muneera, but Muneera had put all the keys of the school in one of the drawers in *Abla* Hessa's desk.

The wife of the janitor, who did the work of her husband inside the school during the day, was sent away with three key chains to find the suitable keys and open the secondary entrances.

The whining of the siren continued.

Finally, *Abla* Hessa was able to reach one of the people in charge at the main administration office. The man calmed her down, nothing to worry about he said, but just to be on the safe side she should gather the students in the schoolyard; they shouldn't in any case return to the building. At the same time, he would notify the fire department.

Abla Hessa sent the teachers to collect all the students in the schoolyard.

The ear-splitting sound of the siren drowned out the voices of the students and the teachers. Nobody knew exactly what had happened and what was going to happen. Why didn't the siren stop? Maybe there actually was a fire somewhere, undetected.

Now Albandary took charge. She instructed the students standing next to her to leave the school, even without their abayas, which were still in the classrooms, to cross the street, and to ask the neighbours to let them in.

But the janitor refused to open the school gate.

Susie stood among the students in the schoolyard. She didn't know what to do. She decided to keep smiling, hoping that her smile would convince the students that the situation wasn't threatening.

The air was hot and dusty. The yard was crowded with students and teachers who didn't know what to do. The whining sound from the siren and the loud voices of the students were nerve-wracking, Susie thought. Why didn't they invent sirens with pleasant sounds, so people could stay calm even if the situation was fretful? Susie concentrated on smiling and breathing slowly and deeply. She instructed the students to do the same. Next to her, one of the students fainted, but her friend kept her from falling down. One girl had a bottle of water, so they sprayed some water over the girl and rubbed her forehead with the water until she regained consciousness.

"Teacher, is there really a fire? Are we going to die?"

"No, there is no fire. Don't be afraid. Soon, the fire engine will arrive. You'll see; tomorrow we'll all laugh about it."

Finally, the janitor agreed to open the gate. Some of the girls crossed the street and rang the bell at a neighbouring house.

They could hear the fire engine as it was arriving. Two men in uniform with long black beards entered the school. They kept their eyes on the ground and asked which way to go, without looking up, until they reached *Abla* Hessa at the entrance to the administration. In the meantime, *Abla* Hessa had taken her abaya from her office and had put it on.

The firemen checked the school for fire, however they didn't find anything. Finally, they turned off the siren.

From *Abla* Hessa the firemen learnt about what had happened. They were shocked when they heard that teachers had advised the students to leave the school without their abayas and without covering. They told *Abla* Hessa that it would have been more honourable for the girls to die in a fire than to go uncovered on the street.

The teachers looked at one another. They wondered if *they* had daughters and sisters they'd be willing to so sacrifice.

After the firemen determined that there was no fire, and it was only a malfunctioning siren, the main administration office instructed *Abla* Hessa by telephone to return the students to their classrooms and to continue with the lessons.

By now, it was nearly noon and the school day was almost over.

Abla Hessa decided to ignore the instructions of the main administration office.

But because she didn't have the authority to send everybody home for the day, she didn't insist on the teachers to continue the lessons.

14.

The next morning, everybody was excited as they came to school.

"Did you read the newspaper? They wrote about us."

"They only mentioned that the siren was broken and that the fire engine came to school. They want to reassure the parents", Albandary replied.

"My brother studies at the university. And the students there were saying that all the students and the teachers had left the school, took taxis, and then met with men at a mall", Fatin said.

"That was an experience", Abrar declared. "Imagine if there had really been a fire. Then we all would have died. See how important it is to pray regularly and to obey Allah. Allah tested us yesterday."

She continued: "We listen to the devil much too often. He whispers in our ears, causing us to be dissatisfied and to treat our husbands with disrespect. Also, we have to stop gossiping."

"Don't always put everything on the devil" Muneera replied. "We've the right to be dissatisfied from time to time. We shouldn't always take all the blame quietly."

"Hey, Rajah, what do you think?"

Rajah was sitting at her desk, smiling, lost in thought. In front of her was an open magazine.

"Me? *Al hamduli Allah*, everything turned out alright. Here, look at this picture. Do you think this hairdo would fit me? What do you think – should I dye my hair blond?"

"No, not blond. Put in highlights."

"Don't you want to order some take-out food? We should celebrate because everything ended well."

A woman of an unspecific age entered the teachers' room. Her face was still covered with the veil, only her eyes were free.

"*Salam alaikum.* Can I talk to you for a moment?"

"Come, *Khala*, sit with us. Do you want some Arabic coffee, Aunt? What can we do for you? Do you have a daughter in our school?"

"No. It's something else. I need your help. My husband died a year ago, just after we moved here from southern Saudi Arabia. He wanted our children to have a better education, and as you know, that's difficult in a small village. We don't have any relatives here and now I don't know how to pay the rent. My oldest son works at a supermarket in the afternoon, after school, but even that is not enough. I've tried to find some work, but as you know, it is difficult to find anything suitable."

"Can you read and write?"

"I went to school for a few years. But then I had to stay home because my mother got sick and I had to look after her and my siblings. I don't have any certificates."

The teachers looked at one another.

"*Khala*, can you come back tomorrow? By then we'll have collected the money for your rent. And we'll ask around to see if we can find suitable work for you, but … you know how it is. Have you considered getting married again?"

"I don't know. Then what will happen to my children?"

"We'll see what we can do. And we'll ask the imam of the mosque if he knows somebody who would be willing to marry you and look after your children. As you know, Allah has allowed a man to take more than one wife so that he can take care of widows and orphaned children. Think about it. And come back tomorrow. We'll see what we can do for you."

After the woman had left the room, Nura said: "*Al hamduli Allah*, we have our job and if it is necessary, we can provide for our children.

We all have good lives, even if we sometimes think that it's all too much. See how important an education is? We should discuss that with our students instead of letting them memorize what's written in the book."

Susie met Hanan, the beautiful girl who sat in the last row, after the break, as she was on her way to her class.

"Hanan, may I talk to you for a moment?"

"With me? What is it, teacher? I don't have time", Hanan answered suspiciously.

"What about your notebook? Where is your homework?"

"My homework? I didn't understand what our homework was."

"And what about the hearts you drew in your notebook?"

"Hearts? What kind of hearts? I don't understand you; your Arabic is not good." Hanan started to become aggressive.

"I know. I thought about not talking to you and letting another teacher get involved but … There are these drawings of hearts in your notebook with *H*'s and *A*'s in it."

"Ah, those are the drawings of my little sister. She must have taken my notebook and scribbled in it. They have no meaning."

"Hanan, you are a nice girl and you're pretty. I want you to take care of yourself. Don't let anybody take advantage of you."

"Teacher, I don't know what you're talking about. Nobody can take advantage of me. Is there anything else? I have to go to my class. Our religion teacher gets angry if I'm late." With these words, she left Susie and went to her class.

15.

Rajah sat in the furnished apartment that Essam had rented for the two of them and waited. Essam had phoned her at school, telling her that he had taken the afternoon off to be with her; he would come following the afternoon prayer. So she had phoned her brother to tell him that she would be with Essam and asked him to pick up her daughter after school.

For four whole days, Rajah hadn't seen Essam. He had phoned her once only to tell her that he missed being with her but that he had too many social engagements and a lot of work.

As usual, her brother's driver had picked up Rajah from school, but then she had told him to drive her to her apartment. On the way she had briefly stopped to buy some candles and a few groceries. She wanted to cook for Essam.

As soon as she arrived in the apartment, she started cleaning and preparing the meal she wanted to share with Essam. She took a shower, put on some make-up, and got dressed. She chose the short black skirt and the see-through red blouse that according to Essam looked so good on her.

She burnt some incense to give their home a beautiful smell, then she looked around. She was satisfied with the way everything looked; the apartment now had some personal touches.

When she heard the call to the afternoon prayer, she quickly performed her prayer. She was ready for Essam.

Rajah turned on the TV and waited.

In the first month after their marriage six months ago, it had always been Essam who arrived first in the apartment. They had agreed that he would bring the food, but then they hardly ever ate together, they were much too preoccupied with each other in other ways. Sometimes he would bring her small gifts – a gold necklace, a bracelet, or some perfume that he liked.

She woke up as she heard the call for the evening prayer.

Finally, she heard his footsteps at the door.

"I'm so sorry, *habibti*, my love. But I couldn't come sooner. Are you upset?"

He looked so handsome as he stood in front of her. Her heart started to beat faster and her knees trembled.

"How can I be mad? I had such a strong longing for you. Why didn't you call?" Rajah asked.

"My mother-in-law! She came suddenly for a visit", Essam told her. "I went home after work to check on the children and there she was. My wife was home, too. I don't know if they suspect something. They were so nice. Strange."

Essam took her in his arms. "But now I'm with you. Come, let me show you how much I missed you."

Later that night he drove her back home.

"When do we see each other again?" she asked as they arrived at her house.

"I don't know. I'll call you, I promise! Not again will I wait so many days until I see you."

Rajah entered her apartment in the house she shared with her brother. Everything was dark. She went to her daughter's room, it was all quiet. She listened to her daughter's breathing. Carefully, she touched her hair and kissed her on the forehead. Immediately, her daughter woke up.

"*Omi*, my mother, are you back? I was waiting for you."

"What did you do today? How was school?" Rajah asked.

"Nothing special. I'm happy that you're back. Come, sleep next to me."

Rajah laughed happily. She undressed, put on her nightgown, and slipped under the covers next to her daughter, who snuggled up to her. Before long, Rajah heard her breathing deeply and regularly.

16.

Even before Susie entered the teachers' room she could smell the freshly baked bread somebody had brought.

"Susie, come eat with us", Huda called to her. They were all sitting around the breakfast table, which was covered with dishes of food.

"Today we celebrate. Muneera has invited us. She has bought all this delicious food."

"Why? What is the occasion?" Susie asked.

"Do you remember – Muneera told us about her sister who studied medicine and was looking for work? They've accepted her in one of the public hospitals and they'll even train her to become a specialist in women's diseases. Isn't that great?"

"Congratulations, Muneera. Now the only thing that's missing in your sister's life is a bridegroom", Susie told her.

"My sister says that she doesn't want to get married – if she has to, maybe to a physician like herself", Muneera replied. "She says the divorce rate among doctors is very high; who wants to marry a woman who is always on call? What if the man demands that his wife stop working? My sister says that she didn't study all these years to hang her certificate in the kitchen! But she knew all this before she started with her studies. For sure she knows what she wants."

They were interrupted by Nura's voice. She was sitting at her desk, talking on the phone. It was clear that she was frustrated. Finally, she hung up and came to the table to join them.

"Why are you upset, Nura?" Albandary asked her.

"Oh, I hate these men", Nura replied. "My son has problems in religion. You all know the verse in the Quran that says that men are our guardians and responsible for us. My son has asked me if that means that men are superior to women. I told him that the verse means that men and women complement each other, they each need the other, and the advantage of one shouldn't be a disadvantage of the other."

"We know that; so then, what happened?" Abrar asked.

"A few days ago, my son got his evaluation – satisfactory in religion", Nura continued. "My son never had any problems before. I always go over his homework with him and make sure that he understands everything. But the teacher confused my son. During the examination, my son wrote the interpretation that I gave him. The teacher didn't like my interpretation; he thinks men are better than women. 'He should write what I have taught him', the teacher wrote on the test. Yesterday, I finally succeeded in sending my husband to the school. Naturally, I can't go to a boys' school, women are not allowed in there. My husband talked to the teacher, but it didn't help. He came home from school and said that this teacher was great, best teacher ever, a pious man! He told me I should let him do the teaching and not interfere."

Abrar said, "Okay, then listen to him."

"No, it's not working. After school, my son comes to me. '*Omi*, help me'. Should I say no?"

"Let your husband study with him", Fatin suggested.

"He doesn't have the time. He comes home at night when the kids are sleeping", Nura said. "Therefore, I have just now phoned the school, the director was nice, but the teacher refused to talk to me. He said he doesn't talk to women. I'm afraid that I'll lose my son to the men's world. If I don't help him now when he needs me, he'll never come to me in the future when he needs help."

"You cannot change the way boys have to be brought up", Albandary explained to her. "Your son must become a man and learn to get respect. Your husband cannot enter his daughter's school and you cannot enter your son's school. Your husband can not be part of his daughter's life and you cannot always be part of your son's life. This is the way it's done. If you always try to solve your son's problems, his personality will become weak, and then the other boys will ridicule him. And you know what that can do to a child."

"I know you're right, all of you. And I'm proud of my son", Nura said. "I always tell him, 'You're a man, you're responsible for your sisters.' A few days ago, we went shopping. I was looking at some gold necklaces, but didn't recognise the design. I lifted up my veil a little bit. You should have seen my son, he was so angry with me that I showed my face. I was so happy; he's really on his way to becoming a man."

"You see?" said Muneera. "He'll make his way. Give him time to play with his male cousins and his friends. If he's among men or boys, he'll learn to become one, too."

"It's so much easier to raise girls", Abrar said. "Just bring your daughter up with love to the Holy Quran; teach her to forgive, to do well. Show her how to become a good wife who obeys her husband, and how to become a good mother."

"Do you really think that I should teach my daughter to obey her husband?" Muneera asked, unbelieving.

"Yes, that's our religion", replied Abrar. "Only when your husband asks you to do something that's forbidden in Islam, that's *haram*, are you allowed to say no."

"Those are interpretations of Islam that we learnt in school, but the reality looks different", Rajah considered. "I know many women whose personalities are much stronger than those of their husbands. Those women knew exactly what they wanted at the beginning of their married life, and then, in the end, the husbands didn't have a choice but to submit to the wife."

"Good, emancipated women", Muneera laughed.

17.

In the morning, Hanan exited the school bus along with the other girls. The street and the school entrance were crowded with girls dressed from head to toe in black. Carefully, Hanan let the other students pass her by. She went around the street corner; it was ten minutes to seven. Nobody seemed to notice or to care; they all wanted to reach the school as soon as possible so as not to get rebuked for arriving late.

Hanan saw his car parked at the end of the school wall. He had told her that he was driving a silver-grey Lexus. Slowly, Hanan walked closer towards the car and was about to pass it. The window next to the driver's seat was open. She heard her name being called.

"Hanan, it's me, Ali. Come, get in."

Hanan went around the car and got in next to him. She held her schoolbag tightly.

"Are you afraid? You don't need to be frightened. It's me, Ali, your *habibik*, your love. As I told you, we only meet to know each other better. We don't do anything bad. Today I'll go to your father and ask for your hand in marriage."

His voice calmed her down. She put her bag, which today was empty, on the car floor and sat back in the seat.

"Where do you want to go? Do you want to drive around?" Ali asked her.

Hanan nodded her head, and he started the car. They passed

the school gate. The janitor, who was usually sitting at the gate, was nowhere to be seen. The gate was closed.

Hanan took a deep breath. Everything seemed to be normal.

Ali drove for some time, neither of them speaking. After a while he parked the car in front of a doughnut shop.

"What is your favourite kind? Or you want me to choose? Do you want a cappuccino?" he asked.

Her friends had often talked about different kinds of doughnuts and cappuccino, but she had never tasted either.

Ali returned with the hot coffee and some doughnuts. He handed them to her and then continued driving.

After a few minutes, he drove into the parking space of a big supermarket and parked the car between several others.

"I think nobody will notice us here. Come, let's share our first meal together", Ali told her.

He carefully took the tray with the coffee and the doughnuts; then he gave her one of the cups and let her choose what she wanted to eat. She thought for a moment before she uncovered her face and began to eat and drink. Ali watched her but didn't say anything.

While she was eating, he began, as he often did, by talking about their common future and how great their lives together would be. After they'd finished their coffee, he suggested they go shopping. "You know that I live with my mother and I promised her I'd buy some cheese and olives. Come, you can help me", he said.

Slowly, Hanan began to get her confidence back. He was really a nice man, she thought, the way he cared about his mother. He would never treat her badly.

The first time she had talked to him was by chance. It was late at night; she had tried to study but had found it difficult to concentrate. She didn't feel like studying or sleeping. Everything was always the same: going to school, eating, praying, and sleeping – every day the same routine.

Before her parents had gone to bed, they had fought, as usual. Her mother had criticised her father, saying that the money he gave her was not enough to support a family.

Now the house was very quiet; she was the only one awake. Suddenly, the phone rang. A friendly, pleasant male voice asked for Abdullah. She liked the voice and answered in a friendly way that there was no Abdullah there.

After that he called her up every night. If by accident somebody else would pick up the phone, he would ask about Abdullah.

Hanan had never before talked to a man other than her brothers or her father. She had often wondered what other men were like. Her mother usually didn't talk nice about men, and the women she knew would always say that a girl should not get involved with a man. "Men are dangerous creatures driven by their instincts", they would say. Talking to them was the first sign of danger. "A girl should only listen to her father, her brothers, her uncles, and if she is married, to her husband. Every other man means danger." It was the duty of a daughter to protect herself; the honour of the family depended on the virginity of the girl.

But Ali was different. He was nice, polite, and always tried to protect her. Hanan was sure: the women who were talking about how dangerous men were didn't know Ali or men like him.

Hanan thought it was her idea to meet; she wanted to see him. Ali had always talked about marriage and how much he was longing to spend his life with her. Her friend in school with whom she had discussed each and every call she ever had with Ali had warned her. If anybody found out about her meeting with Ali, she would be punished severely. Just a week ago, there was an article in the newspaper about a girl the employees of the Commission for the Promotion of Virtue and Prevention of Vice had caught with a man other than her husband in a car. The man and the girl had to go to jail and were severely whipped as punishment. It had been a scandal.

Then, her friend continued, even though Hanan knew a little bit about Ali's life, he was still a stranger to her. Who could guarantee that everything he said was true? But her friend agreed to cover up for her in school and tell anybody who asked that she had just gone to the toilet.

Ali suggested they stop by his apartment so that they could put the cheese and the olives into the fridge, and that way Hanan would also meet his mother.

Hanan agreed. She liked Ali, his behaviour, and the way he talked and moved; he seemed like a man who knew what he wanted. This was the man she had always dreamt of, he was so much not like her brothers.

Ali stopped the car in front of an apartment building in a secondary street. Hanan didn't know where they were. She covered her face again and followed Ali inside the building. Her heart was beating fast as he opened the door to the apartment with his key.

"*Omi*, my mother, where are you?" he called out as they entered.

Nobody answered.

"For sure my mother just went to see her neighbour. Come, sit down. She'll be here in a minute. Take off your abaya", Ali suggested.

Reluctantly, Hanan did what she was told. She didn't feel comfortable. As she looked around, she noticed that the apartment seemed cold, nothing was lying around, no personal stuff – it didn't look like an apartment a woman lived in.

In the beginning, when Ali started to kiss her, she liked it. But then his kisses became more demanding. Hanan became frightened. She asked him to stop, but he didn't listen. She tried to get out of his grasp but he was stronger and didn't let go of her. He opened the buttons of her school uniform and started caressing her breast.

"There, listen, steps, I hear steps", she said. He let go of her. She used the moment to catch her abaya and rushed out of the apartment.

On the stairs, Hanan put her abaya and veil in order and left the building with trembling knees.

She didn't know how to get home. And her bag? She had forgotten to take her schoolbag. Fortunately, the bag had been empty except for two notebooks and some pens. Just then she remembered that in the morning her mother had given her some money to buy a sandwich at school. She touched the pocket of her uniform – the money was still there. She walked along the empty street; nobody was there. Everyone was either in school or at work.

At the main road, a taxi driver stopped next to her. She told him to drive her to school. At the street corner close to the school, she got out and mixed with the students who were about to go home.

Al hamdulil Allah, thanks be to Allah, she thought: the school bus hadn't left yet. She entered the school so that the janitor would not catch her standing in front.

A teacher sitting behind the gate asked her where she had been and why she had entered the school from the outside, but Hanan told her that she had been in school all day and had only checked to see if the driver was outside.

"Okay, but next time, don't leave the school. Let the driver call out for you", the teacher said.

"Thank you, *Abla*, there will be no next time. Never again; I'll never leave the school again", Hanan replied.

18.

Nura looked at her watch: 12:20, only ten minutes until the final bell.

She locked her desk, picked up her purse, and went downstairs. Inside *Abla* Hessa's office, a few teachers were sitting, ready to go home. Muneera was there, Rajah, Latifa, Fatin, and the German, Susie. Susie seemed a little bit lost, as usual. *Does she really know what she got herself into?* Nura thought.

Fatin was whispering with Rajah, who laughed and poked her elbow at Fatin.

"Are you telling jokes again?" Latifa asked.

Rajah suggested going to the school gate; it was time for the janitor to open the gate.

They put on their abayas. Nura had bought herself one of these new abayas that looked like a tent and was closed in front unlike the usual ones that looked like a black cloak with sleeves. She put on her veil and then exposed her face.

Together they left the school building, but the school gate was still closed.

"Abu Mohammed, father of Mohammed, open the gate!" they called out.

But the janitor didn't open the gate. Through a crack in the gate, they could see him. He was sitting on a chair, talking to some of the fathers who had come to pick up their daughters.

After five minutes passed, Abu Mohammed got up and opened the door. Quickly, Nura covered her face and left the school, together with eight hundred students and teachers.

Nura's driver was waiting outside the gate in his car. Nura got in and immediately they drove off. Nura relaxed in her seat. She was tired. With a smile, she caressed her big belly; two more months. Would it be a girl this time?

She started to fall asleep. Suddenly, she was awakened. The car had stopped in front of a red traffic light. Nura heard the screeching of brakes. As usual, somebody had crossed the street by red. *Why doesn't anybody punish those guys?* she thought. It was known that in Saudi Arabia more people died on the streets than in bed. Nura was grateful that she had a good, safe driver.

When she lived with her husband in the States, she had insisted on learning how to drive a car. She had even persuaded her husband to let her take her driver's licence. She enjoyed driving. In the States, there were rules for driving, and everyone seemed to follow those rules. But in Saudi Arabia? Often Nura would see twelve-year-old boys driving the big family car.

As she arrived at her home, Nura told the driver to pick up her sons from the boys' school and then go to her daughter's school. Furthermore, she told him that she was going to meet with her sister at 6 p.m. and so he shouldn't leave the house at that time.

Inside the house, the maid told her that she'd already cooked *kabsa* and that they were out of milk and salad. Nura instructed her to send the driver to the supermarket when he came back with the children and she could then serve lunch to them.

"And wake me up when 'sir' comes so I can eat with him."

Nura went to her bedroom and a few minutes later fell into a deep sleep.

19.

Reham was convinced she had to take action. In the past weeks, she had more and more realised that she didn't want this life; she didn't want to spend the days cooking, cleaning, watching soap operas with her mother-in-law, and waiting for her relationship with her husband to get better. The only highlight of her day was the time she spent with Dahlia. But often when she was with her she became impatient and had to restrain herself from crying. Frustration took over her thoughts and made her moody and irrational.

She decided to talk once again to Bandar; maybe this time it wouldn't escalate into another fight. At night, after she'd put Dahlia to bed, she found him sitting alone, without his mother, in front of the TV.
"I want to talk to you. Could you please turn it off?" she asked him.
"What is it now? What do you want? Another one of your fights?"
"I can't live like this. I'm suffocating. Won't you help me?"
"What does it mean 'I'm suffocating'? Why are you so dramatic?"
"I'm not happy. I feel my life is empty. I want more."
"You're just an immature child. I don't know what came over me when I decided to marry you." Bandar looked at her with contempt.
Reham couldn't bear his expression, it made her furious. "Why?

Because you're so old and wise? Why don't you try to understand me?"

"All I want is to spend a nice quiet evening at home, read the newspaper, watch some TV, and go to bed."

"That's not what I want to do every day! There must be more to life than that."

"Believe me, I have had it, you don't need it. It's enough for you to take care of your daughter."

"But I want more. If you can't give me what I need, I will leave you."

Bandar looked at her in disgust. He sighed.

"Okay. If that's what you want, I'll divorce you. But in return you'll give up Dahlia. She's my daughter, too, and I don't want her to grow up with you, you're a bad mother."

Reham started crying.

"I know that I'm not a bad mother. You always treat me this way. Why do you despise me?"

"Because you always make life miserable for me. Decide what you want and tell me."

With these words Bandar got up and left the room. He regretted the day he first laid eyes on her.

"I hate you, oh, how much do I hate living with you!" Reham shouted.

20.

Muneera entered the teachers' room. She looked tired despite the fact that the day had just begun. Her colleagues wanted to ask her why she hadn't come to school the previous day, but a glance at her face kept them quiet.

During the break, Muneera went to sit at her desk. All the questions, why she didn't come to eat breakfast with them as usual, she left unanswered. Finally, Abrar was able to talk to her. Muneera said that once again she had had a fight with her husband. She was disappointed that her relationship with him had turned out so different than what she had anticipated before they got married.

Two days earlier, after she and her husband had eaten supper, she had tried to talk to him. She was longing for intimacy, she wanted them to spend a romantic evening together, without the computer, but he had told her that when he was sitting at the computer he was actually earning money.

"I don't need more money, we have enough to live comfortably", Muneera said to him. "I want to spend more time with you."

But this he refused.

Muneera was hurt. "Money, always money, that's all you like to talk about."

At this, he reminded her that previously she had refused to share her income with him.

"But that's *my* money! You don't have the right to ask me for my salary. You're responsible for supporting us", Muneera told him. "When I give you money to share with the expenses, I do it to help you, but you can't force me to do so."

A word from her, an answer from him, and soon they were fighting. Finally, he blurted out, "You're divorced."

She packed up some of her stuff, woke up the children, and told the driver to bring them to her father's house.

Her parents were shocked and angry that she had allowed the situation to escalate.

Since that night, Muneera hadn't heard from her husband. She was desperate; she didn't know how to act, what to do. The children asked about their father constantly. Muneera was happy to stay with her mother, but at the same time she wanted to be in her own house, around her stuff. She felt that she didn't belong in her parents' house any longer, her children were too noisy, and even though Muneera's parents were happy to have them around, Muneera felt out of place and with her children a burden to her parents.

Bit by bit, the teachers learnt about what had happened to Muneera. Every time they got new information, Nura told Susie about it. They were all sympathetic toward Muneera because there was hardly a teacher who had not experienced the sorrow a divorce brought to the family. But this was a new incident for Susie; she didn't comprehend how a simple quarrel could escalate in such a way that, in a matter of a few hours, it resulted in a separation. Nura explained to her that a first and second divorce could be annulled easily as soon as the two parties involved had realised that they had made a mistake; but the third divorce was final. Only then could the wife not return to her husband.

"And what happens to the wife if she gets divorced?" Susie asked.

"She returns to her parents", Nura explained. "If the husband is nice, he leaves the children with her. But according to the religious law, he gets custody of the daughters when they're seven-years-old. The sons stay with their mothers and when they are around eight years old they can choose who they want to live with."

Susie doubted that in a matter of hours a marriage could be dissolved. But Ahmed confirmed this information; he also explained to her that there was a waiting period of three months to determine if the woman was pregnant; at the end of this time, the divorce was valid.

For Susie, once again, some of her illusions were destroyed. A few days ago she felt that despite everything she had started to become part of her environment. But this new experience showed her that she was a long way from being culturally integrated; there was too much that she didn't understand or didn't want to accept. For Susie, a marriage was communion, built on feelings that were supposed to last a lifetime, not a functional association of two businesses, made valid by a contract.

Nura laughed: "Don't forget that these laws are 1400-years-old. We follow them and we think that they're better than the love affairs of the Western world. Love comes and goes, but responsibility and contracts are binding."

21.

When Susie returned home from school at noon, she found a long letter from her friend Christa, who lived in the US. For a long time Susie held the letter in her hand, reading it over and over. Then, when she was sure everyone at home had lain down for their naps, she sat down to answer it.

My dear Christa,

Thank you very much for your last letter! It got here just in time – I needed you very much.

You ask how I am. Where should I start?

Do you remember all those long hours we spent sitting at your kitchen table discussing my future? When you gave me all those suggestions for how I could solve my problems? I know that your suggestions were well meant. You are older than me, and your husband is American, so you have gone through many experiences that I probably still have to go through. A marriage to a spouse from a culture other than your own brings many problems that you can only solve when you're sure about your feelings. How often did we sit together and you explaining to me what it is like to be married to an American. But Saudi Arabia is not America.

So many things here are totally different from Germany or even America. In America, things seem to be the same as in Germany. Only when you look closer do you see that things are different. And here, things don't even seem at all the same as in Germany. Here everything is totally different.

Even before I left Germany, I decided not to compare things but to try to understand. Like you told me: to live in a culture other than your own can be enriching when you try to understand this other culture. Over and over, you've told me not to diminish customs that are strange to me. You were right; but it's so much easier to diminish than to try to understand, because when you try to understand another culture, you first of all have to know your own culture and you have to know yourself.

Many times I'm in doubt about myself and I ask why.

But I decided to take this path and I feel I have to live by my decision. It's not that life is impossible here; no, not at all, and I'm happy to be living in a big family. It's only that everything is different from Europe and different from what you know in America. Sometimes I feel like I'm in a television show: the people around me are participating in a soap opera and everyone knows the script except me, I don't have a clue what's going on. I know that one day I'll understand, and then the script will be my life, too. I want it to be my life because I like the people and the culture. But right now I don't feel that I'm getting it.

I need patience, as you've advised me when I talked to you about my decision to marry Ahmed and to follow him to Saudi Arabia. Right from the start you told me that I chose a road that is difficult, sometimes thorny. And you also said that one shouldn't turn around and lament each thorn, do you remember? Who knows, maybe at the end of the road the outlook is indescribably beautiful and very satisfactory.

I'll try to continue on my road. I know that you'll be sitting at the kitchen table, sending me the strength to go on.

Yours truly,
Susie

22.

Gradually, the weather started to change. After the annual sandstorms had stopped, it was even cool enough in the morning to put on a jacket from time to time. Only at noontime it was still too hot without air conditioning.

It was nearly noon now; the noise in the corridors was almost too much. *Abla* Hessa had a meeting with her administration employees, and the students used the opportunity to leave their classrooms and walk around. Susie didn't have a class, so as usual she corrected notebooks. Suddenly, she heard her name being called.

Hanan stood at the door; it was not allowed for a student to enter the teachers' room. She waved to Susie and asked her to step outside.

"Hanan, I'm happy to see you. I wanted to talk to you", Susie said. "I'm more than satisfied with your performance in class these last few days. And your homework – it's always there."

"Teacher, I want to thank you."

"Me? Why?"

"A few weeks ago, you talked to me. That was very nice. You told me to take care of myself. On that day I didn't understand what you meant and I was rude to you. Thank you for your care. And I'm sorry."

"I'm happy that I could be there for you. And if you need anything, come to me. Okay?"

"Okay, Teacher."

After not really feeling like herself during the previous two weeks, Muneera now seemed to be getting a grip. She even began to tell jokes again, even though most of her jokes were about the inadequateness of men.

On Saturday, after the weekend on Thursday and Friday, she was absent again, but then she came back on Sunday, happy and smiling. It seemed as if the old Muneera was back.

She told the teachers that finally, on Thursday, her husband had gone to see her father. He came accompanied by his brother and had brought a beautiful gold necklace as a reconciliation gift for Muneera. After the men agreed on everything, her father called Muneera and asked her, in the presence of her husband, if she wanted to return to him. Muneera agreed, but only under the condition that he would spend at least one hour every day with Muneera and the children.

Her husband had showed sincere remorse. There was gossip going around that many people had lost lots of money by investing in the stock market, and Muneera suspected that her husband was one of them.

Her husband had agreed to all of Muneera's conditions and even volunteered that he was fed up with working on the computer and company shares. From now on, he would spend his free time with his family.

On that same day, Muneera returned home with her husband, but only after her father had a sincere talk with both of them. He told them that a divorce was an earnest matter; even the Prophet had often talked about how much Allah despised it.

Also he advised them to use wise judgement in case differences between them recurred, that they should think about the well-being of their children and not to let a quarrel escalate.

Muneera's mother agreed to look after the children for a few days so the two of them would have an opportunity to make up.

23.

Again, Mona was late for school. When she entered the school building, the attendance sheet had already been removed. Mona had to go to *Abla* Hessa's office to sign in the designated book there. She tried to remember how many minutes she had already been delayed this week. At the end of each week the minutes were added, and then at the end of the semester the minutes were subtracted from her salary.

As had happened so often before, she couldn't get out of bed. Why should she? It was the same every day, only more routine. Mona felt that her whole life took place at school. There were a few years in between when she had studied English at the university, but that wasn't so different from school, either. Later she had returned to the school system and it was the same, almost no modification; the only change was that now as a teacher she didn't have to wear a uniform and she could wear make-up. Mona had always hated the grey, wide uniform; everybody looked like a huge mouse. The students' hair had to be pulled back and was not allowed to fall into their faces. *Why isn't there any individuality?* Mona thought. *There's too much force that only superficially results in discipline. But this discipline lasts only as long as there's an authority figure close by. The discipline doesn't become part of a person's inner life and isn't used by the students for their benefit. If the students had acquired discipline, their willingness to learn would have benefitted from it.*

One of Mona's students was waiting at the top of the stairs.

"*Abla*, why are you late again? I was afraid you wouldn't come today", she said.

"It would be nice if there were no English lessons today", Mona joked.

"I did my homework and I prepared the lesson so you'd be pleased with me. Since you've been teaching us, I like English."

Mona laughed: "That makes me happy. But, quickly, go to your classroom or you'll get into trouble."

There was the smell of Arabic coffee in the teachers' room. *Exactly what I need now*, Mona thought. Fatin, Susie, and Abrar were sitting at the table, so Mona took the seat next to them.

For days Mona had not heard from Osama. The last time they had talked he had told her that their relationship couldn't go on this way anymore. He didn't want to see or talk to her without her family knowing about it. Mona realised that Osama meant everything to her and she missed his evening calls.

Also, Osama had told her that he wanted to ask a sheikh for advice and to inquire if he had the religious right to marry her. If the sheikh agreed, he would then go to Mona's father and talk to him; either her father would agree and they would get married or Mona would never hear from Osama again.

"Mona, what's the matter? You look kind of sad", Fatin asked.

"What do you think if a member of a tribe marries a man who doesn't belong to any tribe?" Mona said.

"How can anybody leave the community of his tribe only to get married? The tribe is your security; your tribe is there for you when you're in need or if you have problems. In our tribe, no woman is unprotected; we're always there for one another. I'd never leave my tribe for any man", Fatin explained.

"What do you think, Abrar?"

"I think the tribe is not as important as the belief in Allah", Abrar said. "We should evaluate a man on his piety. Does he go to the mosque to pray every day? How does he treat other people? That's what the Prophet told us to do; he also said that a father should choose his son-in-law according to his sincerity in his belief, he didn't say according to his tribe."

Fatin contradicted her: "What you say looks nice in our religious books, but that's not reality, and most people today don't see it this way. Also, when a man grows up in the same milieu, folks more or less know about his character. I think that in marriage it's more important that a couple has the same background than if they marry because of certain emotions. Love will develop sooner or later."

"What about men – can they get married to women outside the clan?" Susie asked.

"That's in general no problem; that happens often. In this case, the children become clan members according to their father."

The bell rang; the second period was starting.

That afternoon, outside of his regular routine, Mona's father was at home. He called Mona and her mother to sit with him; after they had drunk tea together, he explained to them that a young man had come to his office at the university to ask for Mona's hand in marriage.

"I got a very good impression of the man. He's educated and has a good position with a very good salary. He said that he's the brother of one of your friends, Mona. But he has one great disadvantage: he doesn't belong to any tribe."

"Didn't you immediately refuse?" Mona's mother asked. "What is the family going to say if we marry our daughter to a man who has no roots, who doesn't belong to a tribe?"

"Mona, I ask you: what do *you* want?" her father asked.

"My friend talks all the time about her brother; I know that they come from a good family. His parents are law-abiding people, I respect them very much. We've known the family for many years. Mother, you know the mother and you like her; she's a friend of yours. I'd like to marry him."

Her mother got angry: "Yes, I like the mother, but not all families I like would I allow my daughters to marry into. What about your sisters? Who will marry them when people hear that you've married a man who's not of our kind?"

After that she refused to talk about the subject again. For her, the case was closed; her answer was no.

Mona's father didn't say anything, he kept quiet. And nobody brought up the subject again.

The next week, the mood in Mona's parents' house became bad. Mona's mother ignored her as much as possible. She was angry that her daughter had even considered marrying a man without descent. Mona's father still didn't say much, but Mona didn't see him that often. She didn't hear from Osama, either, and Osama's sister avoided talking to Mona about the subject of marriage.

One day, Mona's father came home late. Mona was still awake, so her father took a seat next to her.

"Do you still want to marry that man?"

"Yes, I do. I feel comfortable with his family, with his mother and his sister. You know when a woman gets married she spends lots of times with her mother-in-law. We know the family for almost twenty years, they're good people."

Her father told her that in the previous weeks, he'd asked around about Osama; he went to the mosque where Osama usually prayed, then he went to his work, and finally to Osama's uncles. They all confirmed to him that Osama had a good character, was diligent, and a good Muslim.

After that, Mona's father went to his own brother, because as Mona's uncle he had the right to marry Mona to one of his sons. But in the end, her uncle agreed that Mona was no match for his son – their ideas were too different. Furthermore, his son preferred to marry a simpleminded woman who would bear him lots of children and take care of the house and the kitchen. To change Mona into that kind of woman would be nearly impossible.

Next, Mona's father went to the tribal elders, and after a lengthy discussion, they gave their consent to the marriage, but reluctantly. One of the main reasons for granting their permission was that Mona had become too old for marriage to most of the single tribesmen; at almost thirty years of age, she was, from their point of view, an old spinster.

It was agreed that Osama would pay twice the amount of the usual dowry. This money would be put in a banque account, as an assurance for Mona in case of divorce or if Osama should die suddenly.

Finally, the road for Mona and Osama was cleared. The marriage contract was signed in Mona's parents' house. Only Osama, his parents, and siblings, and the closest relatives of both families were present.

The *maazoon*, the religious magistrate, came. Osama, his father, and Mona's father had worked out the marriage contract, which was signed by the men. Mona's brother signed as witness after he made sure that Mona agreed on all points, as it was not customary that women signed their own marriage contracts. The women stood behind the door, secretly leaving it a crack open. The moment Mona's brother signed, Osama's mother shouted with joy and took Mona into her arms, kissing her and calling her "my daughter".

It was decided that the wedding party would take place in the summer, just after the school examination. Because now, after the signing of the marriage contract, Mona and Osama were legally married, Osama came regularly to visit the family and sit with his father-in-law. Mona's father had also given his permission for the two of them to call each other on the phone, a huge step in the tradition of Mona's tribe, where it was common that the groom would see his bride for the first time only on their wedding night.

Osama promised Mona that they would spend their honeymoon in Florida, since Mona had so much wanted to see the West.

24.

"Where is Huda? Does anybody know why Huda didn't come for two days?" Abrar asked.

"That's odd; usually Huda is never absent. I hope nothing serious happened", Rajah said.

Fatin laughed: "Maybe she got married."

At the break, Nura told them that Huda's older brother, Maher, had died in a traffic accident. They all knew that Huda lived with him, ever since their parents had passed away. The teachers decided to go to Huda's house after school to express their condolences. Susie wanted to join the teachers but she didn't know how to behave.

She asked Nura.

"Say '*Athama Allah Ajriq*'", Nura told her.

Susie tried to repeat the phrase but she wasn't very successful. The teachers answered her attempts with a smile: "Maybe it's better for you not to say anything or they'll all start laughing", they advised her.

"What does it mean?" Susie asked.

"It means 'We ask Allah to increase the reward of the bereaved in paradise and to give them patience because they experience pain and grief."

Abla Hessa knew where the house was, and so after school they went with their drivers to Huda's house.

As they entered the property, children playing in the yard told them that the women's entrance to the house was on the right side, for men it was on the left.

The main door was open because all day long, neighbours, friends, and family had been coming to give their condolences.

In the women's living room, black-veiled figures sat on chairs that had been placed around the walls. The voice of a sheikh reciting from the Holy Quran could be heard. From time to time one could hear the keening sounds of a woman, but aside from that the room was quiet. Even children's voices couldn't be heard.

The teachers started on the right side of the room, lining up to give their condolences to the bereaved. At first, Susie didn't recognize Huda; she was without make-up, her eyes red from crying, and she looked so much older. As Huda saw her friends, she started crying again, hugging them, not wanting to let go. Next to Huda sat a youngish-looking woman dressed in black. Huda introduced her as her brother's wife. Huda still talked about her brother in the present tense, as if he was still alive. Then she realised what she had said and started crying again.

Abrar took the seat next to Huda and talked to her softly.

One of the women there told them that the day before, Maher was on his way to work. He had stopped in front of a red signal light and started driving as the light turned green. He was already in the middle of the street when a car coming at high speed from the left crashed into Maher's car. Huda's brother died on the way to the hospital.

Huda's sister-in-law was home with two of her children when it happened. Huda, too, was at home; she hadn't gone to school as she had a doctor's appointment.

Nobody could comprehend how Maher's life had ended so suddenly. That very morning he had teased Huda, saying that the doctor would give her an injection and his little son would hold her hand so she wouldn't cry. They had made plans for how to spend the weekend. And now, all their lives had changed.

Maher was buried on the same day.
Suddenly, everything was different.
What were the women going to do?

After a week, Huda returned to work. She looked sad and tired. All morning long, teachers went to her, taking her into their arms, trying to console her.

The condolence visits had lasted for three days; then life returned to normal, but for some people there was no "normal" life any more. It was Allah's will; Allah had decided that on this day, at this hour, the life of this man should end, and so it had happened.

But what about Huda?

Because Maher's children were still small, Huda's sister-in-law decided to return with her children to her father's house. Her son wasn't old enough to be his mother's guardian, and she couldn't and wouldn't live alone in the house where she had lived with her husband.

As Huda was not married, she had lived in her brother's house after her father had died. Now, with her brother, too, dead, for the first time in her life Huda felt desperate. She decided to live with her younger brother and his wife. She didn't like his wife and his wife didn't like Huda, but where else could she go? Huda realised her situation – she was only a woman and she needed a guardian to live with.

Two weeks later, Huda got a call from her uncle, the younger brother of her mother. He lived in a small town, around three hundred kilometres from Riyadh, with his wife and his twelve children. He begged Huda to come and live with them. She would have the opportunity to teach in a secondary school there.

Huda agreed immediately. She was tired of city life. She had always liked the small farm of her uncle – as a child she had spent many vacations there. She loved her nieces and nephews, especially Little Huda, who had been named after her. And who better to teach the children and to motivate them to learn than an in-house teacher from their own family?

So it was time to distribute the inheritance. Huda was eligible, after Maher's wife and children, but because the children were small they were not permitted to sell the house. The house would be put on the market for rent, and Huda agreed that the income would go solely to Maher's wife and the children.

Then it was time to say good-bye. It was difficult for Huda to leave Maher's children, who carried her brother's blood and his name. She had spent the last six years with them; she knew all their little peculiarities and their aversions; she couldn't imagine going to bed without bidding them goodnight.

But this had been Allah's will.

25.

As the bell rang for the sixth period, Susie got up and went to her class. The corridor was crowded with girls walking arm in arm or standing in front of their classroom, waiting for the teacher. Susie's classroom was empty so she waited in front of the doorway. A student from the classroom next door passed by, smiled sarcastically, and said in Arabic, "Your students have a computer class. They're probably late."

By then Kholoud arrived. She apologised for being late and explained that the computer teacher had kept the students longer than anticipated. Slowly, the other students came to class, stalling for as much time as possible before they had to listen to another lesson. And Susie waited at the door until all the students had arrived and taken their seats. There were still two students missing. Kholoud volunteered to check the restroom for the missing girls. Finally it was time to start the period, but the students couldn't concentrate and seemed disinterested. In response to Susie's teasing, they only gave her tired smiles.

It was hot in the classroom, and as the lesson drew to an end everybody, including Susie, was happy.

On their way home, Ahmed, who had picked her up as usual, told her that the two of them had an invitation. By chance Ahmed had met up with Abdul-Aziz, who had studied with him in Germany.

When he told Abdul-Aziz that Susie lived in Riyadh too, he insisted that they should come in the evening to meet his family.

Ahmed suggested that Susie wear a long skirt and a blouse with long sleeves to show her respect to the wife of Abdul-Aziz, whom he had married after his return to Saudi Arabia. While in Germany, there had been long discussions between them, and Abdul-Aziz had always insisted on his point of view: that an arranged marriage between two people from the same culture was more successful than a mixed marriage.

Abdul-Aziz was very polite and seemed happy to see the two of them. He immediately started to speak to Susie in German. Then Fardous, his wife, entered the room. She had covered her hair and greeted Ahmed from afar before kissing Susie on both cheeks. Fardous had not put on any make-up and she was wearing a loose galabaya.

Because Fardous didn't know any German, the two men spoke in Arabic. Susie got bored, and as Fardous got up to go to the kitchen, Susie asked if she could go with her. Fardous agreed, and so Susie helped her prepare the supper and set the table. Fardous wanted to use the dining table, in honour of Susie's first visit to their home.

"Are you happy with your life?" Susie asked while Fardous prepared the salad.

"Yes, *al hamdulil Allah*, Abdul-Aziz is a good man. He always tries to be virtuous; he gives me my rights and he looks after his parents and his sisters when they need him. When I saw him for the first time in the house of my parents, I liked him immediately. You know, Susie, he's a man you can rely on, a man who always tries to guard his family. Abdul-Aziz gives me security; I feel protected and I don't need more to be happy."

Three small girls were watching television in the adjacent room. Next to them was a baby in a playpen.

"Are those your children?" Susie asked.

Fardous laughed and shook her head.

"The boy in the playpen is my son, Mohammed; Abdul-Aziz named him in honor of his brother. Those girls are the nieces of

Abdul-Aziz, they live with us. Their grandmother is too old to look after them, and here in Riyadh schooling is much better than in the village where the grandparents live."

"Why do they live with you? Where are their parents?"

"Didn't you meet Mohammed, the brother of Abdul-Aziz, in Germany?" Fardous asked.

Suddenly, Susie remembered that she had heard about Mohammed. He had studied medicine, and while he was still a student he had got together with a German woman. Susie had never met them, but Abdul-Aziz had talked about the two often. Susie remembered that Helga had not been an easy person to get along with.

"But why are the children with you? Where are the parents?" Susie insisted.

Fardous began to tell her a long story but she talked very fast and used some expressions that Susie didn't know. Not to show her incompetence, Susie nodded her head from time to time, but she had to admit to herself that she hadn't understood most of what Fardous said. Finally, Fardous said, "Talk to the girls, for sure they'll be happy to hear some German."

Susie went over to the girls and sat next to them on the floor.

"*Guten Abend, ich bin Susie. Wie heisst ihr?*" she said. The oldest girl, who was perhaps six, immediately put her arms around her sisters. She looked at Susie with suspicion and answered in Arabic, "I'm Leila, that is Salwa, and the little one is Rania."

Susie put out her arms and Salwa came to her. She sat down in Susie's lap and cuddled close to her. Leila said something to her, but Salwa shook her head and held on even closer to Susie. Rania turned around and ignored Susie. Susie tried to talk to Leila, but Leila responded cautiously. Susie noticed that Leila didn't know how to deal with the situation.

At this moment, Fardous returned; she said the supper was served and she asked Susie to follow her. Salwa didn't want to let Susie go, so Susie picked her up and carried her along to the dining room.

When Ahmed saw Salwa, his eyes became sad. He tried to talk to her, but Salwa buried her head in Susie's breast and didn't listen. She only opened her mouth from time to time so Susie could feed her.

Only after they were finished eating and Salwa was fast asleep was it possible for Fardous to take her out of Susie's arms and put her to bed.

Susie and Ahmed said good-bye to their hosts half an hour later, but not after they had agreed to repeat the visit.
Fardous kissed Susie, insisting that they would see each other again.

No sooner were they sitting in the car than Susie asked Ahmed about the girls.
Ahmed told her that Mohammed and Helga had got married in Germany and that the two older girls had been born there. Three years ago, Mohammed decided to return to Saudi Arabia; he was longing to live in his home country, to work as a physician, and to help his fellow countrymen as he had always dreamt about. He wanted to live close to his parents and wanted his children to grow up in his hometown. Helga didn't want to disappoint her husband, and so she had followed him to Riyadh. But soon after their arrival in Saudi Arabia, Helga noticed that she was pregnant again. All her pregnancies had been quite difficult, but this one was even more so. Helga couldn't keep any food in her stomach and she suffered from the hot weather.
After Rania was born, Helga developed a strong depression; everything was too much for her, she became apathetic and lost a lot of weight. As Mohammed began to fear for the well-being of his wife, he agreed to send her back to Germany for a while. But Mohammed didn't want her to take the children and fought furiously with his wife. Weighed down by her depression, Helga said good-bye to her daughters; she knew she couldn't stay.

Mohammed, his mother, and the maid all took turns looking after the girls. But whenever Mohammed talked to Helga on the phone, she refused to come back to Riyadh. She told him that she was still depressed and just the thought of Riyadh caused an anxiety attack.

Time passed, and the girls seemed to grow accustomed to the absence of Helga. Leila took over the role of the mother when the three of them were alone, while Salwa would spend lots of time looking at photos of her mother and asking the same questions about her, over and over.

Then suddenly, three months ago, disaster struck. On his way home from the hospital, Mohammed had a terrible accident and died a few days later. Abdul-Aziz was able to talk to him before he passed away and promised his brother that he would care for his nieces like they were his own daughters. That was the reason why Leila, Salwa, and Rania were living in his house. He felt bound by his promise and didn't want to send the children back to Germany; their upbringing was his responsibility. And Helga, more so now than ever since the death of her husband, felt incapable of living in Riyadh.

While Ahmed was telling Susie what had happened to Mohammed, she saw the girls' faces in front of her. She didn't know what to do: should she try to visit the girls regularly to talk to them in German? But maybe that would be too painful for the children. Perhaps it would be better to let them forget the past and let them learn to live like other Saudis. Susie thought it must be difficult to be reminded every day that their own mother wasn't there, a mother who in the eyes if her daughters had deserted them.

Susie asked Ahmed to talk it over with Abdul-Aziz and to let him decide if he wanted the girls to learn German or not.

26.

"*Salam alaikum*, good morning, how are you?" Susie asked as she entered the classroom.

"Teacher, we're tired. We feel like a data banque – somebody feeds us with information, which we've to save and then during a test we spill it out again. It's frustrating", Kholoud complained.

"Where's Wafa?" Susie asked.

"She's with the social worker because there's a bed in her office; Wafa didn't feel well, she fainted, so we took her upstairs. You know that she married some time ago", Kholoud added.

"I thought that today we'll do something different", Susie said. "Do you remember yesterday we talked about the word *wealthy*? I want you to get into groups of five. Get out a piece of paper and write a paragraph together: "I want to marry a wealthy husband." Are you against it or for it? You've got the whole period to write. When you're finished, I want you to give me the paragraph."

To start out, Kholoud had to translate the title. Then an intense discussion ensued. They had discussed all the necessary vocabulary the day before, but naturally most of them had already forgotten the words. Quickly they formed into groups of those who agreed and those who disagreed with the theme. Susie promised them that she would correct the paragraphs, and after the students had rewritten them they would post them outside the classroom wall for everybody to see and admire. Some of the students volunteered to put some drawings with the display, and they all wanted to sign their names to what they had written.

At the beginning of the next period, a woman Susie had never seen before was standing at the doorway to the classroom. She was dressed in a skirt and a blouse and introduced herself as Maha, inspector of English. She apologised for being late and explained to Susie that usually she came twice a semester to check on the teachers. They entered the classroom together and after Maha found an empty chair, she sat down. Susie started with the period and soon forgot that there was a visitor in the classroom.

Five minutes before the end of the period, the inspector left the classroom after telling Susie in English that she wanted to see her in *Abla* Hessa's office. There she gave Susie an evaluation sheet of her performance in class and told her to sign it. After Susie read it, she refused to sign.

"What you wrote about me is not true", Susie complained. "I've tried to call on all the students in the class, but there are only forty-five minutes in a period and fifty students in the class. I can't call on each student. And I corrected the notebooks, but some students didn't give me theirs – they said that they had forgotten to bring them. So what should I do?"

"You have to be strict with the students", the inspector said. "If a girl didn't bring her notebook, give her a minus point; the students are taking advantage of you. They come to school to learn, not to feel comfortable. In front of Allah, you're responsible for what you do in your periods and how you treat the students."

"It is because of what you say that I've got to be kind to the students; there shouldn't be any force in learning or in religion", Susie answered.

"Do what you want, but sign. I've a lot of work and no time for discussions."

In the meantime, Latifa had entered the office. She had heard the last sentence and gave Susie an indication that she should sign the paper.

"Sign it and then do what you want", Latifa whispered. "*Abla*

Maha comes twice each semester and gives orders. We always say "yes", and then she leaves again. There is nothing she can do except talk and give us orders."

"But if we're always quiet and never object, then nothing will ever change", Susie told her. "The school system will never be improved, everything stays as it is."

"I personally don't want changes", Latifa said. "Who knows – maybe what comes is worse than what we have now."

Reluctantly, Susie signed the paper and said good-bye to the inspector.

The next day, as Susie was about to go to her class, Kholoud and another student were waiting for her in the corridor.

"Teacher, this is Gamra", Kholoud said. "You know her; she sits next to the window. Can she talk to you?"

"Gamra, what can I do for you?" Susie asked in Arabic. Kholoud stood by in case she needed to translate.

Gamra told her that her English was bad; she didn't know the letters of the English alphabet and she couldn't read. Susie realised that without knowing the alphabet it was impossible for a student to learn English. So she arranged with Gamra that they would meet for additional lessons whenever Gamra and Susie were free.

They started meeting on a regular basis, on Saturdays and Tuesdays, during the last period, in an empty corner in front of the teachers' room. Susie taught her the alphabet, then she practised reading and dictation with Gamra. Soon, more students came to these lessons, as Gamra would often bring a friend. Now they needed a room for their meetings. Finally the physics teacher agreed that they could use the lab, but only as long as nobody touched anything.

During some of their lessons, when it was just the two of them, Gamra told Susie about herself. Her mother had died when Gamra was still a little girl. Her stepmother had brought her up, but in exchange she had to help with the household chores. When she was fourteen-years-old, her father married her off to a much older man; he didn't even ask her if she agreed, since there would be one less mouth to feed.

Gamra's husband had two other wives; he was nice to her but she wasn't happy. After they'd been married almost three years, her husband passed away, but Gamra didn't feel sad. In the meantime, her father, too, died, so Gamra moved into her brother's house. Her sister-in-law was happy to have help with the household and the children, but Gamra wanted to go back to school, she wanted to pick up from where she had left off before she got married. She insisted that her brother give his consent because she couldn't enroll in school without his approval.   Unfortunately, Gamra was not always able to do her homework, especially on the days her sister-in-law needed her help. The one subject Gamra really had a problem with was English; she had forgotten the alphabet, and when she saw a written page in the book she frequently panicked.

It was at this point that Susie came to teach at Gamra's school. Since Susie spoke to them only in English, Gamra felt even more lost than before. She started to hate the days when they had an English lesson. She got the idea of hiding out in the restroom, but that was not a solution, since somebody would always find her and send her back to the classroom. One day, Gamra decided to ask Kholoud for help. Kholoud defended Susie.

"She's different from the teachers we know", Kholoud told Gamra. "She doesn't know that you don't understand her. Go and tell her. If you want, I can go with you."

After that, Gamra started to watch Susie. She thought that maybe Kholoud was right. Susie seemed friendly. Gamra had never before seen a woman with blue eyes and light-colored hair. Susie also was tall, much taller than the women Gamra had known. Gamra watched Susie's behaviour; sometimes her voice became impatient, but most of the time she smiled. Gamra felt that she didn't understand what the teacher said, but she decided to give Susie a chance.

Whenever the students would complain about Susie and argue that she was so different, Wafa and Kholoud would defend her. One day, a student saw Susie in the market. She was wearing an abaya, but it was not fixed on her head, she wore it on her shoulders, and she hadn't covered her face. The description of Susie in the market resulted in a fierce discussion until, again, Kholoud defended her.

"She shows her face but she's not wearing make-up. Everybody can see her – that means she doesn't do anything *haram*, sinful, so she's not afraid. And she's German. We cannot expect her to share our traditions. Leave her alone. She's nice to other people; that's what Allah told us to do", Kholoud said.

With that, the discussion ended for some of the students; some others went to *Abla* Abrar to talk to her. Was it acceptable that the German teacher showed her face in public? *Abla* Abrar told them there was a record that had come down from Aisha, the Prophet's wife. She had said that when she performed the pilgrimage together with the Prophet, the women would cover their faces only when men passed by. This was interpreted by some sheikhs to mean that women should cover their faces, whereas this saying was taken by yet other sheikhs as a proof that women do not need to cover their faces because of the Arabic word that was used for 'cover'. Some people believe that the *khimaar* covers the head and the face, whereas linguistically the word only means a head covering.

"But", *Abla* Abrar continued, "she's still new here, we have to be patient with her."

Gamra felt she could trust Susie. During the extra lessons, Susie would sit next to her, waiting patiently until Gamra had deciphered the words. Gamra didn't feel as helpless as before and became more self-confident.

"Teacher, I'm so happy that you teach us", she told her. "Please, stay with us next year and help us get through the government examination. Then I can work, and my sister-in-law and my brother cannot order me around anymore. I know that if you help me, I can do it."

Susie smiled. "*In sha Allah*, Gamra – we'll both do our best."

27.

"Do you know that today we're alone for the first time in weeks? What are we going to do?" Susie asked.

Ahmed didn't answer.

"I know: I'll fix us something nice to eat, and then we'll watch a movie together."

Ahmed still didn't answer.

"What is it? Don't you feel like it?" Susie asked.

"I feel like it, you know that, but I have to talk to you first."

"Why? What about?"

She looked at his face. He looked tired and it was clear that there was something important on his mind. Lately, he often looked like that, but Susie had always put the reason on his work or the family.

Ahmed had changed since they had come to Riyadh more than three years ago. He had less time to spend with her, and the evenings that they used to spend alone had become a rarity.

Susie followed Ahmed into the sitting room and they both sat down on opposite armchairs – *like two strangers who are here for a visit*, Susie thought.

"Zainab has found a wife for me."

"What!?"

"They insist on me getting married", Ahmed said. "You know, my mother always says that she wants to see my children before she dies. Now that we've already been married for several years and still don't have children, my family is getting anxious."

"But we went to the doctor and he said that there is nothing wrong with me."

"Yes, nor with me. But what should I do? Without children, who will carry my name, what is the purpose of life? The purpose of life is for the family to go on existing. My mother doesn't want my name and the name of my ancestors to die with me."

Susie didn't know what to say. For weeks she had felt that there was something in the air; she'd had a presentiment of a coming disaster.

"I thought that you loved me", was all she could say.

"Love? This has nothing to do with love", Ahmed replied. "This new marriage has no meaning; always my people have taken a second wife when there were reasons for it. We are not the first couple to have to deal with that. I have to think of my mother, this is what she wants. It's difficult for me to refuse my mother her wish."

"But what about me? Is it easy for you to do that to me?"

"You want to stand on the same step as my mother? My mother is very important to me and her wishes—"

"I'm not important?"

"Yes, you are, but it's different. I'm an Arab."

"I know that you're an Arab", Susie snapped. "I have left my country to live with you, not to share you with another wife."

"You don't share me with another wife. You'll always be important to me", Ahmed tried to calm her down. "You and I, we have gone through so much together and we've always been there for each other. Do you think I'll ever forget that? But this is different, it's for the family. The other woman was married before and she's proven that she can bear children. She's divorced, but her sons live with their father."

"I cannot share you with anybody. When I think about you lying in bed with another woman, smelling her hair, caressing her body like you do mine, that in those moments she's in your thoughts more than I am, no, I can't do that! We belong together, that's what you've always said."

"Yes, we belong together. That I marry another woman, that's only an act. It has nothing to do with the two of us. In many other cultures people have these acts and their women accept them for what they are."

"But I'm German, for me this is different, that's the way I was brought up. I would be tormented if I had to share you."

"What about your father? He practically had two wives. How is that different? I'd divide my time equally between you, as is common in my culture. I'd come to you every second day and then we'd have time for ourselves. For the other woman I would rent an apartment. It has nothing to do with you; it would be as if I were away on business."

"No, I cannot do that. I'm not my mother. On the day you get married, I'll return to Germany. That's my last word." At that, Susie got up and left the room.

28.

After the fourth period Susie was free, so she started correcting tests. To help the students, Susie had arranged with them that she would give them a quiz each Wednesday, the last day before the weekend. The girls knew that the monthly examination would come from these questions. So a student who was weak in English but who was determined to pass only had to study the quizzes. Even so, the students still complained that Susie was too strict in her correction; for them it didn't make a difference if *night* was spelled with a *g* or not.

The other teachers in the teachers' room had their heads together, whispering as usual. But this time it seemed that something important had happened. At that moment, Albandary came to Susie and told her that *Abla* Hessa wanted to see all the teachers who taught the eleventh grade of the literary section, and that Susie should come with them. Susie followed Albandary and the other teachers into the office. Some of them, including Abrar and the social-worker of the school, were already there in *Abla* Hessa's office.

Abla Hessa closed the door to her office, insisting that everybody must keep the discussion they were about to have confidential. Then she told them that the two teachers who had *monawba* duty the day before had caught two students, Hajer and Asia, in an immoral act. They had been lying on one of the carpets spread outside, covered with an abaya. The two teachers had watched them for some time and found that something fishy was going on under the abaya. In the past there had been similar complains about Asia, but nobody had given it any attention.

"As we all know, it's normal at their age for girls to develop feelings for one of their peers. But I think this time it has gone too far", *Abla* Hessa told them. "The question is, what we should do? We don't want too many people to know about it – this is a delicate affair, and we don't want to destroy the girls' future, because that would happen if people were to learn about it. All of you are teaching these two, so what do you suggest we do?"

"They have to be punished, severely and immediately. Their behaviour is sinful, we have to stop them, the sooner the better", Albandary said.

The psychology teacher contradicted her: "I agree with *Abla* Hessa that we have to solve this matter wisely. I know Hajer well; she often comes to talk to me. She never mentioned her inclination towards women but I suspected it. Hajer has many psychological problems. I suggest that we send her to a psychologist."

"Today, in the morning, I phoned the mothers of the two girls to tell them that I needed to talk to them", *Abla* Hessa told them. "Hajer's mother is divorced from her father and she rarely sees her daughter. I noticed that her mother is very anxious. She's remarried and her new husband doesn't like her having contact with her daughter. But she promised to try to come to school. Asia's mother, on the other hand, was not very polite on the phone. She accused the school of having a bad influence on her daughter – that at home, in their family, everything is perfect. She insulted me: we should take better care of our students, she said.

"Asia comes from a very good family. I don't know where she got her inclinations or her bad behaviour", Albandary said.

"We have to discuss what we should do. Should I inform the main office and tell my supervisor? That could have severe ramifications for the girls."

Abrar suggested, "First of all, we've got to lock the toilets. The girls spend too much time there, even though we already removed the mirrors. Who knows what's going on there."

"And if the students have to use it?"

"We lock them all except the toilet on the ground floor. And the students are only allowed to use it with permission, and then one by one."

"But this doesn't solve our current problem", the psychology teacher replied.

Abla Hessa asked Susie, "What do you think about the two girls? You teach them, too."

"Hajer is a difficult student, always interrupting the lessons. But I found out that one can control her if she gets attention and affection. She's intelligent", Susie told them. "You can notice from her behaviour that she doesn't get any love or care at home. Asia isn't that easy to deal with. She's stubborn and only wants to get her way. She always tries to influence other students and get them on her side."

The social worker piped up: "I don't think we should keep quiet. It's possible that some other students noticed what was going on under the abaya. We have to sacrifice the two students to protect the other girls. You have to inform the main office."

"I realise that you are right", *Abla* Hessa decided. "But I'll try to keep it as discreet as possible. I'll contact my direct supervisor."

The next day, *Abla* Hessa again asked the teachers to come to her office during the break. She informed them that she had talked to the two girls. Hajer immediately started crying and confessed, she told them. After that, *Abla* Hessa talked to Asia. Asia disputed everything and then threatened the director.

"I don't permit you to accuse and insult me while I keep quiet", Asia had told her. "You can't prove it. I didn't do anything wrong. I don't know what you're talking about."

Abla Hessa again contacted her supervisor, and they agreed to address the problem discreetly. It was suggested that Asia leave the school the following semester but the administration would not give her a negative report. She was told to study the rest of the current semester as a home student and to only attend school during the examinations.

Because the psychology teacher had pleaded on Hajer's behalf, and after several sessions with her stepmother, it was agreed that Hajer would visit a psychologist. She was allowed to continue school, but every day during the break and after school she would have to stay in the office of the social worker and not mix with the other students.

29.

When the bell rang, Latifa got up to go to her class. She was happy that this year she was teaching the twelfth grade. The girls were working hard; everybody wanted to give her best to get good results in the government examinations, so that they could go to university. The last-year students always realised that they had to be on good terms with their teachers, so they were polite and mostly well-behaved.

In the scientific section, the door to the classroom was still closed when Latifa arrived. As usual, the physics teacher had not been able to finish on time; the girls had probably asked too many questions. For years they had only memorised the material, and now they were faced with problems they didn't understand.

Despite her own sorrow, Latifa couldn't help smiling as she entered the classroom. Not only did the girls look exhausted but their hair was untidy and they weren't even able to reply to Latifa's greetings. Latifa was glad that for today the lesson was going to be easy; they only had to write a guided composition, whereby a given paragraph had to be substituted by new words.

By the end of the lesson, the students seemed to have recovered. After they finished their compositions, Latifa collected their notebooks in order to correct them. Some of the students talked quietly with one another, but some others took out their math notebooks to start their homework. Latifa asked a student to take the English notebooks to her desk and left the classroom early. In the corridor, she met Nura. Latifa noticed that her belly had grown in size; she moved heavily but still there was something else about her: Nura was blossoming. She looked happy. Latifa felt a pain, tightness in her chest.

On the stairs, Latifa encountered a pregnant student coming up from downstairs, and in the schoolyard she almost stepped on a pregnant cat that stretched out, fat and lazy, next to a pillar.

What's wrong with me today? Latifa thought. *Every female being is able to get pregnant, except me. Why did Allah put this strain on me? Why is this my fate? Do I ask too much? All I want is a child and my life would be perfect. The average Saudi bears six children. I can't have even one.*

In the last weeks, Latifa had realised that she had to act. She had been married for ten years. Her marriage was ideal. Her husband, Zaid, was considerate and kind. Latifa had always appreciated that he never made a decision before talking it over with her. She felt lucky that he treated her not only like his beloved wife, but like a genuine partner.

The day before, she had gone with Zaid to visit his sister, who had just given birth to a son. The father had slaughtered two lambs as was done according to the sayings of the Prophet. On their way home, Zaid had been quiet. Zaid's sister now had five sons, and even though money had been scarce, somehow the family seemed to get along, and they had welcomed the newest addition to the family with lots of love and affection.

Latifa had often talked to her aunt, her mother, and her sisters about her problem and asked for advice. Her mother was the third wife of her father. Latifa had grown up with half sisters and with a father who only came to the house every third day. So recently she herself had decided to look for a wife for Zaid. Even though married life with a second wife was not unusual for her, Latifa felt sad and disappointed. She only had two choices, and she had to decide now. She could go on as usual, deny her fate, and wait every month to see if her period came, but this way she might lose Zaid, sooner or later. Or she could face her fate and try to do her best to keep her husband. She knew she didn't want to lose him; she didn't want to spend the rest of her life as a divorcée. She loved her husband and had always wanted to grow old with him. But she couldn't expect her husband to give up on children. Maybe if she would put jealousy aside and look for a second wife, she could keep her husband.

When Latifa first talked about it, her mother got upset; she had always wanted a better life for her daughter. Her sisters advised her not to put her husband's attention on the problem but to wait for him to decide. Only her aunt understood what was going on inside her and advised her to talk the problem over with her husband before she decided on anything.

Because of that, yesterday evening, after they returned home, Latifa talked to Zaid. Deep down in her heart, she still hoped that Zaid would refuse to take another wife, but he surprised her when he agreed to the idea immediately. He even told her that he had already found a suitable bride – he had just been waiting for the right moment to tell her. The wife-to-be was the sister of a co-worker of his; he hadn't seen her yet, she wasn't really a beauty, the brother had told him, and for sure she wasn't as beautiful as Latifa was, but she had been married before and had borne children.

At that moment, Latifa felt grief. Though it had been her decision all along, she felt cheated on. She'd always believed that she was everything to Zaid – the love of his life – and now he'd told her that he'd already made the arrangements without discussing it with her first. From now on she was to share his body and maybe even his heart with another woman. She realised that she'd lived on a cloud of illusions all along.

Latifa entered the teachers' room. She looked at her friends. Albandary corrected notebooks while Abrar performed the noon prayer. Rajah was going through a magazine, while Muneera and Fatin were talking in low voices. Maybe it wasn't that bad that her husband got married again, she thought. From now on she didn't need to cook every day and she would be free to visit her mother and sisters. Zaid never liked her spending time outside the house, she had to be there waiting for him when he came home from work. But under this new arrangement, she would still have a husband and his love but she also had more freedom. If she played the situation right, maybe she could even become a second mother to his children. This was Allah's will; Allah had created her with the deficiency of not being able to bear children. This was her fate, and she had to use the situation in a way that benefited her.

30.

During the break, Arwa saw Hanan in the prayer room. Arwa was surprised – it was unusual to see Hanan there. She and Hanan had attended junior high school together, and in secondary school they had been classmates, in the tenth grade. Then Arwa had decided to go to the scientific section while Hanan went to the literary. From then on they hardly saw each other. Arwa and her new friends were always busy studying; students who were ambitious usually attended the scientific section. Arwa had put her mind on going to university to study biochemistry. She knew that there weren't many places where she could work in this field in Saudi Arabia, but at this time in her life she didn't care about that, she loved the subject. If nothing else would come up, she could still become a teacher even though she couldn't imagine herself working in a school.

Arwa went over to greet Hanan. She was happy to see her. Hanan seemed different. When Arwa asked her how she was doing in school, Hanan told her that the only subject she really faced problems with was English. For much too long she had ignored the subject because she didn't like it and had not studied enough.

"Why? You liked English when we were in junior high; you have always been a good student", Arwa said to her.

Hanan grinned: "The usual reason. I took everything much too easy. Can you help me? You're studying the same stuff we are."

"I'd like to help you, but as you know I have much too much

work. Every second day we have a test; we hardly learn something before they test us in it. There is so much pressure on us. But why don't you go with Gamra to the German teacher? I think she'll help you. As you know, she teaches us, too; she is supportive and she always tells us to come to her if we have questions. Do you want me to go with you to ask her?"

They went together to Susie, who immediately agreed to help Hanan.

When Arwa thought about Hanan, she felt sad. They had been close friends before, but then Hanan started to hang out with other students from her class and spent less time with Arwa. "You're a nerd and a bore", she had once told her.

In the last period, Arwa had physics, but she couldn't concentrate. As usual, the teacher talked too fast and the lesson was too short. The class was supposed to start at 11:45, but the bell did not ring on time and the teacher arrived late, so that the period only lasted thirty minutes instead of forty-five. As she left the classroom, the teacher told them to study the rest on their own from the book. But Arwa didn't understand the teacher, so how could she manage to study from the book? *Why did we never go to the lab as we are supposed to? That would have been fun*, Arwa thought.

When she returned home after school, her mother was sitting in the living room feeding her baby sister.

"Why are you late, my daughter? I've been waiting for you."

"My brothers picked me up late again. Can't you tell them to come on time?" complained Arwa.

"You know that they don't listen to me anymore. Where are they now?"

"They are with father outside in the tent. I think they have visitors."

"Then please go and help your sister-in-law in the kitchen. You know that since she's pregnant, she gets tired easily."

Arwa went to her room and changed into her galabaya, like

her mother and her sister-in-law. She went into the kitchen and together with her brother's wife, she finished preparing the food and the salad. After they had transferred the *kabsa* on the big tray, Arwa called out for two of her brothers to carry the tray and the salad to the men.

In Arwa's family, the men ate together from one tray. It was traditional among many families in Riyadh to follow the example of the Prophet, who used to eat rice with his hands. As usual, Arwa's little brother sat next to his father at mealtime and forgot to only use his right hand while eating. His older brother got upset and disciplined him:

"You're no baby any more. How often did I tell you to eat with your right hand? It's unclean to use your left hand, the hand you clean yourself with in the toilet; and don't forget to only take from what's in front of you. Do I always have to remind you?"

The little brother got up crying and went to the back of the house to the women's side. His mother comforted him, then she put his little sister in his lap and got up to help Arwa so that the women could eat, too.

After she had finished eating and had prepared tea for the men, Arwa began to clean the kitchen. Her mother and sister-in-law came to help, but then Arwa's little sister started crying and her mother left them to feed her.

When she was finished with her chores, Arwa sat down on the floor and started doing her homework. She still was not accustomed to writing on a desk. But she got sleepy; the pen fell out of her hand. She collected her notebooks and pens so that the little ones wouldn't play with them. Then she put her head on the Arabic cushions behind her and immediately fell asleep.

She woke up when her little brother came and told her that the men wanted Arabic coffee. She wanted to complain, but who else would do it? Her sister-in-law was tired from the pregnancy and her mother was busy with the little ones. Reluctantly, she got up. *Why do women always have to do everything*, she thought. *Why don't the men prepare the coffee like it was custom in some other families?* If she ever got married, she would put it in her marriage contract that her husband had to help her, she decided. And he would also have to spend time with her – he would have to sit with her and they would talk to each other. She didn't want a marriage like her sister-in-law's, in which she had to spend the days with Arwa's mother. She wanted to have her own apartment where she would live with her husband.

Finally, she finished the work in the kitchen and went to do her homework. Two hours later, her mother called; it was time to prepare supper.

31.

It was the last school day before Hajj vacation, which would last for two weeks so that pilgrims would have an opportunity to visit Mecca and perform the pilgrimage. The students, and even the teachers, walked around with happy faces.

During the break, the atmosphere in the teachers' room was frisky. Rajah and Fatin sat together, whispering and laughing. Between them, lying open on the desk, was an old magazine whose pages they turned from time to time.

Muneera had taken the seat next to Albandary and Abrar. This year she wanted to perform the pilgrimage with her husband, and she asked Abrar how she should behave while at the holy sites.

The desk where Huda used to sit was still empty. A new teacher had come to replace her, but she'd preferred to stay in the other teachers' room.

After the break, Susie noticed that Nura didn't have a class. She sat at her desk, correcting notebooks. As Susie approached her, Nura put the notebooks aside.

"How are you, Susie? You look tired."

"I'm not really feeling well", Susie replied.

"Why? Do you want to talk about it?"

"It's possible that I won't come back to school after the vacation. I made a plane reservation to go back to Germany."

Nura looked at her, surprised.

"Why? What's wrong? Come, we talk in the kitchen, we'll be alone there, nobody will disturb us."

Susie followed Nura into the kitchen, which was only used by the teachers. Susie told her that Ahmed wanted to get a second wife in order to have children, and that she had informed him that the day he got married, she would leave the country.

Nura listened to her without interrupting. When Susie was finished, she asked, "Where are you going to live? Do you have friends or family in Germany? I know that your parents are dead."

"I don't know where I will go. I hardly have any friends left in Germany, only one childhood friend, and she has her own life. I have a friend in the States but ..." Susie started sniffling. "Since the day I met Ahmed, my life has revolved around him and around Saudi Arabia. I have neglected my friends because they weren't part of his life. But I can't live here if he has second wife, I can't put up with sharing him."

"We are your friends, we all love you, you're one of us. You don't know how much you mean to us", Nura told her. "We respect you because you share our life; you give us hope. If a German can endure our life, it can't be that bad. When we're frustrated, we look at you and realise that life in the Western world isn't that great, either, not like they always show us in their movies and on television. Stay with us, don't go! It's the devil who puts these ideas in your mind. We are your friends, we're your family."

"I know. I have the same feelings about all of you. I feel at home here. But ... I can't ... and ... I only wanted to inform you, so that when I don't come back, you'll know why."

"Please, think about it. Maybe you made your decision too fast."

"I don't think so." With these words, Susie turned around. She knew that if she were to stay there any longer, she would break down. Distressed, she went back to the teachers' room.

32.

Susie looked at her suitcases. Had she packed everything that was important to her? *But what was important?*

Ahmed was important, and he wasn't coming with her.

He had said that he would be back on time to give her a ride to the airport.

Susie felt restless and depressed; she had shed so many tears that now crying only exhausted her and made her more tired and more desperate.

Ahmed had gone with Fatima and Zainab to look at the new wife Zainab had found for him. Zainab had praised her immensely – "a really good opportunity and so pretty." Susie had tried not to listen when they talked about the woman; she pretended not to understand Arabic.

It seemed that Samia didn't agree that Ahmed should take another wife. For the first time, she showed her affection to Susie when two days ago she "talked" to her. She had pointed with one finger at Susie and with the other at Ahmed and then she rubbed the two fingers together and smiled. But then she separated the fingers and shook her head.

But Susie's decision was set: she would not share Ahmed with another woman; she would rather give him up completely.

He had looked so good as he left the house. He was wearing a new *thob* with a black *mishlah* and a new white *ghutra* on his head.

He even smelled good; the room had taken on his smell. Susie took a deep breath: this smell would always remind her of Ahmed.

She went through the apartment to say farewell. Carefully, Susie touched the things that had been important to her. How many happy hours, and some sad ones, had she spent here? How often had she been homesick? And she had thought *that* was her biggest problem. *How silly I have been*, she thought.

Her life here had come to an end, and it had been a short life. And she had come with so many good intentions.

She went to the sitting room and sat down in one of the arm chairs, the same armchair she was sitting in when Ahmed first told her that he was going to get married.

She heard the call for the evening prayer and she sat in the chair without moving.

Then she heard Ahmed's steps. *Strange, he's coming alone, without Fatima and Samia, so I won't be able to say good-bye to them.*

Ahmed looked tired as he entered the room. His face was pale; he hadn't slept a lot the last few nights.

Susie got up: "Ahmed, I'm done packing, we can go."

"You're really in a hurry. Don't you want to know how it went?"

"Why should I? This isn't my life any more, this only concerns you."

"So quickly do you want to get rid of me?"

"I never wanted to get rid of you. You left me when you put the interests of your family above us."

"Ah, the German is speaking. Listen first to what I've got to tell you. Sit down and listen", Ahmed ordered.

Reluctantly, Susie sat down in the armchair opposite Ahmed.

"Okay, I'm sitting down. What do you want to tell me?"

"As you know, we went to see the woman. She's really very pretty, Zainab has really chosen well. She has long black hair and beautiful black eyes. Her face is friendly. When we arrived, my mother and Zainab went to the women, while her brother greeted me. The father was there, too. He was nice, like one imagines a father should be. We talked and we found out that we have the same acquaintances. Soon, my mother and the woman's mother entered the room. The mother said that her niece had once met you at a wedding party. Then the woman came into the room. She's still young. She offered us juice and coffee. They're a really nice family, a man could not ask for better in-laws. Altogether, it was a nice evening. But—"

Susie didn't want to listen any more; she couldn't bear to hear what he had to say. Pain and jealousy took possession of her mind.

"What 'but'? Do I still have to listen to how great that family is?"

He looked at her sadly.

"Why don't you listen to what I want to tell you?"

"Okay", Susie sighed. "I'm listening."

"But as I looked into her eyes, they were black, not blue, and at that moment I knew that I don't want to spend my life with her. I want to look into your eyes when I'm happy and I want to see you when I'm sad; I don't want another wife."

"But what about your mother and your sisters? What about the interests of the family?"

He smiled.

"You wouldn't believe it. As we left the family and were sitting in the car, mother was quiet; for a long time she didn't say anything. Suddenly, when we were almost at Zainab's house, she looked at me and said that she doesn't agree with this marriage. She said that she realised that you are my wife, we belong together, and she said that she loves you like her own daughter. She said, 'Ahmed loves a German woman, that's his life. I already have grandchildren, and so if Allah gives children to Ahmed and Susie, then I'll get grandchildren from them, the will of Allah is above everything.'"

"Did she really say that?"

"Yes, and I realised that I want you, only you. We're partners, with or without children. I want to get old with you. Go, unpack your suitcases, and then we'll watch one of your German movies if you like."

Susie got up. Yes, she would stay. This time she would stay.

About the Author

A German native, Barbara has been residing in the kingdom since the early seventies. She has a bachelor's degree from Washington State University in English and worked as an English teacher at a number of public schools in Riyadh. As her six children have all graduated, she now spends her time accompanying her husband of 40 years on his business trips around the world.